LOVE
FROM
Amanda TO Zoey

Ian Mark

Omnific Publishing
2355 Westwood Blvd., Suite 506
Los Angeles, CA 90064
www.omnificpublishing.com

First Omnific ebook edition, February 2018
First Omnific trade paperback edition, February 2018

Library of Congress Cataloguing-in-Publication Data

Mark, Ian.
Love From Amanda to Zoe / Ian Mark – 1st ed. isbn: 978-1-623422-52-3
1. New Adult Romance — Fiction. 2. Lost love— Fiction.
3. New York City— Fiction. 4. Introspection — Fiction. I. Title

10 9 8 7 6 5 4 3 2 1

Book Cover Design by Amy Brokaw

Printed in the United States of America

Chapter 1

"Will you marry me?" The words hung in the air like a slowly deflating balloon. As soon as I asked I regretted the question, and I knew what the answer would be. To her credit, Amanda took it in stride. Her pencil-thin eyebrows raised ever so slightly in surprise. I glanced away, wondering if any of the other patrons had heard me. Our waiter, Ramon, walked past as I spoke, and our eyes met. I hated him. He'd talked down to me the whole meal, correcting my pronunciation of *arroz con pollo* and flirting with Amanda by complimenting her Spanish. She loved that, just about any compliment would put her in a great mood, no matter how small. That's why I so rarely complimented her.

Amanda continued not to say anything, and I hated silence. I felt the need to fill the air between us. This was not going as expected. I looked her over as she looked me over, and I saw the curly brown hair, the mole just above her cleavage, and the pearly white teeth that were just slightly crooked. She hated wearing her retainer. She tucked her hair behind her ear, a movement she had performed thousands of times in her life, while she prepared to turn down a marriage proposal for (I assumed) the first time in her life.

"I know I don't have a ring or anything, but-"

"It's Wednesday," she said.

"What?"

"It's a Wednesday."

"I know the date,"

"We're eating at *El Cantinero*, where we've eaten at least a dozen times in the year we've been dating. It's a Wednesday night, I've been working all day. You don't even have a ring."

"I love you."

"Don't say that." She seemed visibly upset at the idea.

"I know it's not the most romantic-"

"Not the most romantic? Zach, how could this be any less romantic?" She put down her utensils and wiped her mouth with her napkin. Apparently the thought of marrying me had made her lose her appetite for her Tasty Tasty Tacos.

"Do you even want to marry me?" She continued. She plopped her napkin on her food in front of her. She always did that. She never took her leftovers home. Even if she didn't want them, I would eat them. I always told her that, and she always said, *Next time.*

"Of course. I wouldn't ask otherwise." I cut off a large piece of *arroz* or *pollo*, whichever one means chicken, and ate it while trying to meet Amanda's eyes. My dull brown ones searched for her brilliant blue ones, but couldn't find them. She looked down at her lap before speaking.

"But do you really? Think about it right now. Do you want to spend the rest of your life, some sixty years-" She knocked on the plastic table painted to look like wood in front of her- "with me?"

I considered it. She was pretty, hell, she was beautiful. A little short, but great legs, a nice chest, and a symmetrical face. But she was kind of annoying. She wasn't quite as smart as I was, and she would always talk during movies, asking for clarification or wanting me to repeat what Leonardo had just said. And she snored sometimes when she slept over. Not the kind of snore you could ignore, either. I snored like a normal person, consistently making the same sound so that the person next to me could get used to it and still fall asleep. That's just being considerate. But her, her snores were like a succession of different dying animals calling out, ranging from the low bellows of a wounded elephant to the scared shrieks of a trapped mouse. It was infuriating really. I'd turn over and over again, and no position could get me away from those noises. Even worse, it wasn't every night, so I couldn't prepare for it. We'd be sleeping and everything would be fine, then at 3:23 in the morning I'd hear a whinny, and I'd know I was trapped until six, when I could duck out and say I had to work early.

"No," I conceded, "I guess I don't want to marry you."

She softened. She sank back into the plush red booth and took a sip of her burgundy wine. Ramon brought the check over and glanced at Amanda's mole. *I should punch him*, I thought, before suppressing my primal desires.

"Look, Zach, I know you've been through a lot," she said after Ramon had finished eye-fucking her. She leaned forward and put her dainty fingers over my slightly-less-but-not-as-less-as-I'd-like dainty ones and smiled a sad smile.

"Brian's death is making you recognize your own mortality, and that's *normal*."

I sighed. Amanda was a psych major in college, and even though she worked now in a law office, she never let anyone forget that she took two classes in grief counseling. Misinterpreting my annoyance as another sign of my depression, she went on.

"You're afraid you'll die alone. And you think marrying me will make things better, make you more secure. But you don't want to marry me. We haven't exactly been great the last few months."

A pause. She leaned back and took out her phone. Ah, a text. Much more important than breaking my heart. I finished my Dos Equis with a swig and reached for the check. I slid my card in and looked for Ramon. Of course, now that I needed him, he was nowhere to be found.

"Sorry," she said, "Where was I?"

I looked around the sparsely populated establishment for Ramon. An elderly couple a few tables over looked at me, and I stared blankly at them. *They must be so happy*, I thought. They looked away, and went back to their silent meal.

"You were telling me why you don't want to marry me."

She looked at me, the way she looked at me when she thought I was being intentionally stupid. Most of the time I wasn't, no matter how incredulous she was.

"No, Zach, we were discussing why you don't want to marry me."

"I asked, didn't I?"

"Yes, but you just admitted you don't want to marry me, because this is just an impulsive reaction to Brian and your newfound mortality."

"Yeah, and you snore."

"I what? I don't."

Her brow furrowed. The corners of her mouth turned down. I knew I should leave it there. But I didn't.

"Yes you do. It's worse than any girl I've ever slept with."

"Stop it, Zach." I could tell from her voice that she had heard this before. How many men had complained about it to her? How many ways had she tried to make it stop? I handed the check to Ramon as he walked past, and he almost dropped the tray he was carrying. So sloppy.

"It's awful. It keeps me up even when we're not together, the echoes of it."

"Fuck you Zach," she said quietly. She got up.

"Sixty years of that, I'd probably kill myself." There. The last straw. I broke her.

"You selfish, idiotic, fucking asshole," she said, no longer bothering to keep her voice down. The old farts two tables over looked up, surprised. I waved.

"You don't care about anybody but yourself." Her cheeks were red, and her hair was in her eyes. Her mouth contorted into an ugly snarl. *She's really not that pretty*, I thought.

"We're done," I said. I squeezed a few grains of rice together with my fingers and ate them. She hated when I did that.

"Oh no," she said, almost yelling, "You don't get to dump me, I'm dumping you. You asked me to marry you ten minutes ago. *I* am dumping *you*."

"Okay." I smiled at her. She stormed out of the restaurant. I watched as all the other patrons watched her go, then turned to see what had caused such a ruckus on this quiet Wednesday evening at *El Cantinero*. I watched them watch me. I smiled.

"Show's over folks. I apologize if we disturbed your boring lives."

Ramon brought the check over and grinned at me. He was missing a tooth. I tipped him ten percent. Asshole.

Chapter 2

I lie on the ground. The dirt presses into my back. A voice speaks ominously from somewhere above me. I look left and right. Tombstones. Am I dead? I try to get up and I float in a way that tells me I no longer have a body. The rabbi speaks but I can't understand him. There is no one else there, so I guess he is talking to me. I look down on my dead face. Lightning crashes, and I float away from my funeral. I see Amanda, home with Ramon. My mother and father are eating dinner nonchalantly. I float to the edge of the table that I sat at for so many years. We are in my childhood home, even though they moved shortly after I went off to college. I search my mother's appearance for any sign of distress or sadness at my passing. There is none. I glance at my father, and he is the same, stoic as always. Maybe they don't know. I try to tell them. No words come out of my mouth, because my mouth is miles away in an empty graveyard. The rabbi has left. Two blind men bury me while quoting *Hamlet*. I float to another room and Ethan Hawke is there. He doesn't look at me. He says to his wife, "Isn't it just terrible to die alone?" I try to cry, but no sound comes out. Suddenly, I feel a presence next to me. I turn and Brian is there. He looks at me, his eyes are dead and he doesn't speak. His nose is red. I try to engage him, but he turns and leaves. I follow. We are at a lake. He grabs me, ethereally, and I am forced under the water.

I rolled out of bed and grabbed my phone off my nightstand. 9:47. One new text message: *You wanna grab a beer tonight?* It was from Kevin. *Sure,* I texted back. I found my slippers and trudged to the bathroom. After a luxurious fifteen-minute shower, I looked myself over in the mirror. I looked good. Not too big, not too thin, I had a bit of a six-pack going today and my hair looked sharp. I dressed and was out the door in five. I zipped up my hoodie as the harsh wind hit me. I hated the weather here. I walked the two blocks to the Starbucks on West 4th. I gave a nod to Jimmy, the homeless Jamaican man who hung around there. I pulled open the door and joined the long line of stressed out NYU students. I remembered when I was one of them, just a few years ago. Miranda smiled when I got to the front of the line.

"What'll it be Zach?"

"I'll have a grand caramel macchiato with a double shot of espresso and cream." I winked.

"One large black coffee it is." We both laughed. I thought of something.

"Actually, could I also get one of those scones?"

"Sure." I paid and received my order.

"Thanks, Miranda. Have a good one." I left and removed the scone from the bag. I passed Jimmy and handed it to him. He grinned a toothless grin. He really was an ugly motherfucker.

"Tanks, mon," he said. "God bless you."

"Take it easy, Jimmy," I replied. I shook my head as I walked away. I don't believe in God, and my life's not even that bad. How Jimmy, a homeless man who spent his day being ignored and treated as subhuman by stuck-up college kids, could believe in God was beyond me.

I entered through the revolving doors of 200 Mercer Street and nodded to Marvin, the security guard. The warmth of the lobby enveloped me, and I unzipped my hoodie. I put my hands in my pockets.

"Zaaach," he said, "How's life? How's Amanda doing?"

"Dumped her last night. Soooo probably not too well."

We both laughed, but I don't think either of us thought it was funny. It's interesting, the differences between what we think and what we say when we interact with people we're not that close to. The elevator came, and I nodded goodbye to Marvin. He was already greeting the next yuppie coming in.

I got off at the seventh floor. I worked as a programmer for a small start-up that made social video games. Basically, the founders wished they had come up with Farmville, and were now desperately trying to create the next Farmville so they could profit off the insatiable desire of humans to spend as much time as possible performing strange mundane tasks instead of working.

As a programmer, my hours were pretty flexible. I rarely showed up before ten or eleven, and almost always left before four. I was the fastest programmer there, but nobody knew that. If they knew, I'd have more work to do but wouldn't make any more money.

I checked my email and found my assignment for the day. There was a problem with one of the games I was working on. Apparently the fish in *Hunter-Gatherers: The Game* had been exiting the lakes and "swimming" on land. Easy enough to fix. It took me fifteen minutes to figure out what I was going to do and about an hour to write the code. Then it was onto the internet for the rest of the day. I loved my job, but I also hated it. Sometimes I wished it were more challenging. And everything there was just grey. Grey, grey, gray. My cubicle was grey, the walls were grey. Even, Bob, my nearest coworker, was grey. He was in his early forties, and he worked harder than any of us to keep up. Poor guy didn't grow up with computers. He's grey. He's like a normal person with all the color drained out of him, just faded to grey.

I thought back to a conversation Brian and I had had one day early in sophomore year. Neither of us had any work, so we were playing NHL '09 on our suite-mate's xBox.

"Have you ever seen *Say Anything...*?" Brian's baritone cut over the country music playing in the background as we selected our teams.

"The John Cusack one?" I picked the Bruins and Brian went with the Sharks.

"Yeah." We advanced through jersey selection.

"I think I saw it a long time ago." I waited for Brian to press A to start the game.

"You know the buy, sell, process part?" I looked over at Brian. He was looking at me, not talking at the screen like we normally did. He scratched his chest through the pink v-neck he was wearing.

"Press A." I put my feet up on the edge of my bed and leaned back in my chair.

"What? Oh, sorry." He hit A and the game went to a loading screen. I looked at him again. His hair, while by no means long, was getting to the point where I knew in a few days he'd start talking about needing it cut, and in a few weeks he'd actually go get it cut. "Anyways, Cusack's character, he's asked what he wants to do when he graduates high school. And-"

"He's the slacker, right? And he dates the valedictorian?" The game started. I won the opening face-off.

"Yes, and he says he doesn't want to buy, sell, or process anything for a career. He doesn't want to buy anything sold or processed, sell anything processed, or-"

"Let me guess, process anything bought or sold?" Digital Patrice Bergeron fired a wrister towards Digital Evgeni Nabokov, who caught it in his glove.

"Yeah." Brian went silent for a few minutes. We had a lot of conversations that went like this: eyes always on the screen, long unmentioned pauses, little coherence to anyone but us. "Give it to 'em Joe!" He yelled as Thornton beat Rask stick side high.

"Always go stick side." I started the riff.

"Hell of an effort, you love to see it." Even though I wasn't looking at him, I could tell he was starting to smirk, the right corner of his mouth bending upwards.

"You know, it just looks like the Bruins don't want it enough out there today." I started to smile too.

"Coach Claude Julien irate on the sidelines, calls over his star defenseman Zdeno Chara-"

"He's saying, listen son, I know you're an all-star, but you gotta show all these fans you're one." Brian lost it. He started giggling. I did too. A girl on our floor freshman year had described the way we played these games as "One of you says one word, and you both just start giggling for five minutes."

"So what's your point?" I asked midway through the second period, after we had quieted down and I had restored order to the game. I had a 2-1 lead.

"My point is, I'm just like Lloyd Dobler." Brian answered quickly. He knew what I was referring to, even though we had talked about several other things since he brought up the Cusack movie. "I don't want to do any of those things."

"So you're dropping out and becoming a kick-boxer?" I remembered how the movie played out.

"Shut up, let me finish. I have no major, right? And I figured out today that I don't want to do any of them. I don't want one career, I want to do a lot of things, and what I really want is to act." His normally confident voice got higher here, as if he was asking me what I thought of acting.

"Transferring to Tisch? Don't go all artsy on me now." He scored to tie the game with a few seconds left in the period. We both mashed A to skip through the replays and pause screens to get back to playing as soon as possible.

"That's just it, I feel like it's a waste of money to do Tisch, but I want to be in Tisch. I don't know, don't you ever think you won't wanna do Comp Sci?" I had declared my major towards the end of Freshman year. I didn't love it, but it was practical and I was good at it.

"Not really, it's what I'm good at and there are a lot of jobs." Rask grabbed the loose puck and froze it. While the game went to a replay, I picked up the scissors on my desk and poked my desk.

"Yeah, but how many years can you do the same thing before you wanna quit?" Brian leaned forward and put his feet solidly on the ground.

"I don't know man, I don't know." We both fell silent. I thought about Dobler as the game went on. With a minute left, I said quietly, "What else is there?"

"What do you mean?" Brian asked. He fired a shot and then collected the rebound and shot again. Rask grabbed the puck and I pulled the right trigger to get him to spit it out.

"Well if you don't buy, sell, or process, what do you do?" Thornton stole the pass. The sticks on Brian's controller clacked as he aggressively and quickly turned and fired a shot just under the stick of Rask.

"Create. You can create." I pulled my goalie, but the game was over.

"You wanna play one more?" I looked at Brian. He grinned.

"I'll play a few more."

Stuck in a rut now, I knew what Brian's advice would be. "Why don't you just quit?" He had asked me numerous times. I hated that question, and had been glad in the months leading up to his death when he stopped asking. It was only later that I had two epiphanies: He stopped asking as he withdrew into himself and confronted his failure as an actor, and I hated that question because I didn't have any good answers for it.

* * *

"So you and Amanda split, huh?" Kevin said as I brought over the first round to our usual table at Brad's. I sat down, leaving the chair between us open, a ritual we had faithfully carried out since Brian died a month and a half ago. A semi-cute girl came over and asked if the empty chair was taken.

"Yes," we said in unison. The girl glowered at us and walked back to her more attractive friends.

"How'd you know?" I asked Kevin. Had Amanda called him? Were they closer than I thought? Did they ever sleep together?

"She updated her relationship status."

"Ah." I knew I had forgotten something. Now it really did look like she had dumped me. I hadn't even wanted to make it Facebook official, for this very reason.

"We're just going to break up," I had told her as she kissed my neck and snuggled up next to me. I pulled the covers over our naked bodies and wrapped my arms around her.

"Don't be so pessimistic," she chided me. "I want everyone to know." She bit her lip and looked up at me. She was so damn cute.

"Fine," I said.

"You wanna talk about it?" Kevin interrupted the memory. "Are you-"

"I'm fine." I said. "Let's just get fucked up."

11

"Hey," he said. "You don't need to tell me twice. You done with that?" I sucked down the rest of my Budweiser and nodded. He went to get another round. A busboy came to take the empties. He had a hideous chinstrap beard and a scar across his forehead. I nodded to him and surveyed the bar. As usual, it sucked. Barely any women, and what girls that were there were seated at tables. It's weird hitting on girls when they are sitting down. Creepy, really. I was still stuck in a relationship mindset. I needed a few more beers to get back in the single-guy mindset. Kevin came back with a pitcher and I laughed.

"So what's our game-plan?" Kevin asked me a few beers later. "Let's find you someone to take Amanda off your mind." I laughed. I liked Kevin. He played with the top button of his dark blue button-down and gulped down some beer. I took charge, relishing being single again. When I was eighteen, I arrived at NYU knowing almost nothing about women. I soon learned I had a certain effect on them, and while it still surprised me at times, I enjoyed the benefits of it.

"First off, if you're debating it, undo that." I gestured to the button he was playing with. He did so.

"How's my hair?" He said. I looked pointedly at his crew cut as he ran one hand over it. We laughed raucously. Life was good.

"Sexy as always. Now, this place is dead as usual. I say we hit up Josie's."

"Sounds good." We rose. I went over to the coat rack and grabbed our stuff. I had traded the t-shirt and hoodie for a polo and a pea-coat. I looked at my reflection in the mirror. I looked damn good. I brushed my dark brown hair out of my eyes and smoothed it down by running a hand over the top of it. *One of these days I'll buy a comb,* I told myself. An undergrad nervously looked at me, and I grinned at her. I was warming up. We left Brad's and its poorly lit grungy decor for the just slightly classier Josie's across the street. I pulled a cigarette out and lit it. Kevin frowned. He didn't like me smoking. Cancer, he said. I don't want to live that long anyways, I always replied.

"You don't have to wait for me," I said. We both knew he would. We stood in silence for a few minutes. Finally, I threw down the cigarette. Kevin stamped it out with his loafer. He dressed up for these nights. We went down the stairs and handed our ID's to the bouncer. He nodded to us and we went in. The bar smelled like sex. The mix of perfumes and colognes combined with the stale beer and sweat that was everywhere to produce an aroma found only in bars like Josie's. Everyone here was here to get laid, and most of them would. I went to the bar and bought four shots of tequila. Two girls were sitting at the bar. One of them smiled at me.

"Me and my friend are going to do shots," I told her.

"What?" she said.

"Shots!" I yelled.

"Okay!" She squealed and grabbed her friend to get her attention. They each wore low-cut tops and short skirts. I signaled Kevin over to join us.

"This is my friend Kevin," I said. Kanye drowned me out.

"What?" she said.

"Kevin!" I pointed at Kevin.

"Oh. Carol!" she pointed at her friend.

"What's your name?" I said. I pointed at her.

"Becky!"

"Zach!" the shots arrived. I gave the bartender my card and opened up a tab. We threw the shots back. I caught Kevin's eye. He nodded at Carol. I nodded at Becky. We smiled. We were in agreement.

Chapter 3

I lie in the grass. I stand up and walk over to the track. I am on my high school's football field. I stretch. I head to the starting line. A voice from somewhere announces the results of the last heat and the names of those participating in the current heat. My name is not said, or if it is I do not hear it. I stand in the ninth lane and take my position. Amanda is next to me. She wears neon shorts and a white top. I can see the outline of her breast beneath her top. Her nipples are hard. She does not look at me. A gun goes off. Amanda takes off. I try to as well. My feet don't move. It's like running in Jello. I slowly move my way down the track. The other runners are all ahead of me, and none are as far away as Amanda. She looks back once, right before she wins. We make eye contact. She shows no emotion. I look to the stands. Brian and my mother sit in the highest row. He is eating pure sugar by the spoonful. She is crying. He makes no effort to comfort her. The other runners finish. Brian and my mother get up and leave. I trip and fall. I curse, but no one hears me.

* * *

Morning. A throbbing headache woke me. The hangover was worse than I expected. I wished I was eighteen again. I looked up. For a second I believed I really was eighteen. Same cinderblock walls as my old dorm room. I reached for my nightstand. I didn't find it. I noticed for the first time the girl sleeping next to me. Or on me, really. The bed was so small I was basically pinned between her and the wall.

"Shit," I said. Kate, or was it Becky? She woke up.

"What's the matter?" She said. "Go back to sleep."

"You're a freshman," I said. "You told me you were a senior."

"So?" she said. "It hardly matters now. Go back to sleep."

"I have to go to work." I climbed over her and realized I was naked. And I still had the condom on. I went to the bathroom and discarded it in the toilet. I peed and looked in the mirror. I looked like shit. I walked back out into the tiny dorm room and noticed the Justin Bieber poster above her bed. A wave of nausea hit me. I grabbed my jeans and shirt. I couldn't find my socks. She sat up and watched me. Her dorm was too clean. When I lived here, my dorm was always littered with clothes, smelled like weed, and had beer bottles behind every nook and cranny. Hers was almost sterile. It was like a hospital. The aqua blue bedspread was the only color in the room. Her roommate, who evidently had been made to sleep elsewhere the night before, had a black comforter and black sheets. While Becky (or Kate)'s bed had a headboard, her roommates didn't. It occurred to me that when I had lived in a dorm like this, she would have been twelve years old.

"Where do you work?"

"Small Monster Games."

"You're in the legal department there?" She reached for her phone.

"What? No, I'm a programmer." I found my socks and put one on. The other had a hole in it. I sighed and put it on anyway. She typed on her phone while I talked. She didn't look at me. She was a little chubbier than I remembered from last night. Or from what little I remembered of last night. She had a zit right by her left temple. The makeup that covered it the night before had worn off. Her neck was covered in hickeys. I had way too much to drink last night, I decided.

"So we both lied, then. You told me you were a lawyer." She looked up at me, her brown eyes filled with a strange combination of regret and apathy. I found my shoes and headed towards the door.

"It hardly matters now, does it?"

Amanda's face flashed through my mind as I asked the question. She wasn't impressed by my conquest, but disgusted. I wasn't winning the breakup, I was losing any chance I had of getting back together with her. I recalled bitterly how we got together in the first place…

Shortly after graduation, Kevin, Brian, Amanda and I had crashed a wedding. We had all started hanging out senior year. It was an interesting dynamic. People always assumed Amanda was dating one of us. She was just one of the guys, and we had made a game of tallying which one of us outsiders thought was dating her. I was winning by a large margin.

The wedding was in Brooklyn's Botanic Garden. Amanda wore a shining black dress that hugged her as she gracefully walked away from our table to the bar. The three of us wore black suits, with different color shirts and ties underneath: white and blue for Kevin, blue and silver for Brian, and maroon and black for me. Kevin waited until she was out of earshot, then turned conspiratorially towards us. I watched the bride smiling and laughing as she was congratulated by a procession of beautiful guests. I saw the groom watching her and smiling to himself. Something stirred inside me.

"Are you guys ever uncomfortable hitting on girls?" Kevin's question snapped me back to our table. Kevin was uncomfortable? He had never seemed it. Granted, he normally needed a few drinks in him to get going, but I always figured that was nerves. I waited for Brian to answer. He liked to talk about things like this, various aspects of society that are taken for granted but rarely discussed.

"Not really. Nervous, maybe. But that's what this is for." Brian raised his champagne glass as he talked, scanning the dance floor for lonely bridesmaids. "Why else would you crash a wedding?" He chortled. Kevin seemed unsure. He looked down into his glass. It was mostly full.

"I don't know, Amanda's certainly not here to pick up girls." I watched her order a drink from the bartender. He wore a white jacket and black bow-tie. He nodded and smoothly grabbed a Corona from beneath the bar and popped the top off all in one motion. Amanda took it from him and smiled, then turned to come back to our table.

"I think she has a different reason for being here." Brian and Kevin looked at each other knowingly as a tall black man wearing a blue suit approached her. He placed his hand on the bar next to her and smiled. His teeth were strikingly white, and he had a goatee and mustache combination that would have made Clyde Frazier jealous.

"I guess," I conceded. Amanda smiled back at him. With her mouth at least. Her eyes didn't have the twinkle they normally did when she really smiled.

"Here's how I look at it," Brian declared. "When girls go to bars, they are going out to meet people. They know just as well as we do why we go there." Kevin listened intently. Amanda extricated herself from the man at the bar and picked her way through the tables and dance floor towards us. "They dress up because they want the attention. As long as you listen when they say no, and are polite, there's nothing wrong with it." As Amanda approached, Brian sped up, eager to end the conversation. "I look at it as meeting new people, no lines or ulterior motives. If I make a new friend, great. If I get laid, even better. What'd you get?" He directed the question towards Amanda as she sat down between Brian and me.

"Just a beer."

"You're hardly taking advantage of the open bar," I said. I raised my Long Island Iced Tea. "You gotta get creative."

"I'll keep that in mind. What is that, your second already?" I nodded. "What are you guys talking about?"

"Football," Kevin and Brian said in unison. They nodded at each other approvingly. I sipped from my glass.

"You know what? You're right." With that, Kevin got up from the table and approached a lonesome perky blonde girl wearing a revealing aqua-blue dress and drinking a cosmo. I watched him go.

"I hate hitting on girls," I said, still looking at Kevin. Brian raised his eyebrows, but didn't say anything.

"Really?" Amanda didn't believe me. "*You* don't like hitting on girls?" Brian laughed at her emphasis.

"I really don't," I protested.

"But you do it all the time. And you're good at it." Amanda took a swig of her beer and continued. "It's like if Brian said he didn't like acting or if I said I hated drinking beer. And Zach," she took another gulp of beer, "I love drinking beer."

"I don't like it. It's just that, I, well, I don't-" I searched for the words. I would have had no trouble telling Brian this, but with Amanda there I wasn't sure how much I wanted to admit. "I want a relationship, okay? But it terrifies me. So I do this. But I don't like it. It's creepy." Brian laughed.

"It is not," he said. "They want to be hit on." He sat back, satisfied he had won the argument. I wasn't done.

"I don't care if they do, it's still weird. It's just better, I guess, then trying and failing at having a relationship. Which I know I will." I slumped in my chair. I felt strangely tired. Amanda looked at me with a strange expression on her face. *She pities me,* I thought bitterly to myself, *this beautiful girl thinks I'm a loser.*

"I'm going to go... help Kevin." Brian stood up suddenly. He winked at Amanda and headed over to Kevin, who had moved on from Blondie and was now talking to two similar looking brunettes. Sisters, probably. I remembered that we weren't supposed to be here. If I had any respect for marriage, I probably would have left. But marriage had always struck me as the end of your real life, of being young and having fun. After you got married you had kids then you raised them then you were old and then they put you in a home and it all passed in the blink of an eye and then you needed a walker and then you died.

"Wanna dance?" I asked Amanda glumly. I was too tired to talk to girls. She smiled and offered me her hand. I took and it and led her on to the floor. A slow song came on and Amanda wrapped her arms around me.

"He's right, you know." I felt her breath on my earlobe as she whispered.

"About what?" I asked. We swayed with the music. I looked over her shoulder at the band. The singer had his eyes closed and was holding onto the mic stand with two hands. He was alone with the music. I wished I had a similar passion for my work. I had just gotten my job at Small Monster Games, and the work was easy and rarely interesting.

"About girls. Most of us like getting hit on. It makes me feel pretty." I pulled back and looked at her. She blushed.

"You do know you are pretty, right?" My question made her smile shyly.

"I guess…" I laughed.

"I always used to assume that hot girls knew they were hot. I guess a lot don't. Amanda, you are gorgeous." She blushed deeper. I put my head back next to hers. She later confided in me, that she did know she was pretty. "Guys like it when I pretend not to," she had said. Manipulative bitch.

"You're not too bad yourself." She pulled back and looked me straight in the eyes. The song ended. A fast song started playing.

"I guess we better-" She kissed me mid-sentence. I hesitated, then reciprocated. I cupped her face with my hands. She stroked the back of my neck. I moved my hands around her waist. We stood there motionless, as couples all around us danced feverishly to the fast-paced jam. The singer was bouncing around the stage, mic in hand. After a while, we went back to our table.

"Bout damn time," was all Brian said when we sat back down. I laughed.

"Shut up." Amanda and Brian shared a look. It occurred to me that she had confided in him about me. I wondered how many signals I had missed, how many chances I hadn't taken.

We danced the night away. Kevin and Brian were talking to a couple of beautiful women when we left, though I never found out how it ended. Amanda and I spent the night at her place. She admitted that she'd had a crush on me for a long time.

"I wasn't going to do anything because I thought you were kind of a player." She was making coffee in her red bathrobe. I sat at her kitchen table in boxers. My suit, undoubtedly now wrinkled, lay forgotten somewhere in the bedroom.

"What do you mean?" I watched her work.

"You're always hitting on women, and I thought you'd just…" She stopped.

"Sleep with you and never call you?" I finished her thought. "What changed your mind?" She placed a cup of coffee in front of me and sat across from me.

"When you said you didn't like hitting on people, and that you are scared of a relationship. I guess I thought we could, or would…" She trailed off, looking at me for some confirmation. She wanted to date me, I knew. The idea still kind of scared me.

"Well then, congratulations. You were the target of the longest play I've ever run. I had to pretend not to like it just to get you into bed." She started to look upset, and I stopped the joke. "I'm kidding. Maybe. You'll never know." She still seemed hurt. She got up and turned away.

"You're a jerk." She said it softly.

"Amanda?" She turned to me. "Can I take you to dinner tonight?" She smiled and nodded.

So began the longest relationship I'd ever had. I never really got comfortable opening up to her. I had been telling the truth— I didn't like hitting on girls then, and I liked it even less the older I got. But I still preferred it to the emotional intimacy of a relationship. I was a solitary person, and I figured I always would be.

* * *

I sat in my cubicle at work. I hadn't even pretended to start working when Bob came by. He looked grayer than normal.

"What's up, Bob?" I plugged my phone into the charger. It had died sometime last night.

"Not much, Zach, how are you?" He leaned against the wall of the cubicle and crossed one leg over the other. I logged onto Facebook to see if I had posted anything dumb last night and find out what happened to Kevin.

"I'm alright, a little hungover. Anything I can do for you?" There was nothing of note on Facebook except a notification that Amanda had changed her relationship status. I changed mine to "it's complicated" to be as much like a petty eighth grade girl as possible.

"I was hoping you would drop in on that meeting later, you know, throw your two cents in and whatnot, just to show we're on the same page with this."

"Sure," I said. "Will you email me the details so I don't forget?"

"Course." He pulled at the loop of his waistband. Bob was the kind of guy who didn't like the casual dress code. He was more comfortable wearing a suit than the polo and khakis he wore today and every day. "See you there." He made the short trip to the other side of the cubicle walls. I listened to him sit down. I could picture everything he did even though the wall prevented me from seeing him. Sit down, write a note to himself to email me, cough, take a sip of the shitty coffee from the break room, decide to send the email now, type out the details, sip the coffee, hit send.

I heard a ping. I had one new email. I checked my phone. No calls from Amanda. Three from my mother. I decided to listen to the voicemail she left. It was a long message of little importance. She sounded frail. I hated that she didn't sound as strong as she used to. She was a tough woman, my mother. She used to beat me and my dad in arm-wrestling. He didn't like that. Always said she had an advantage because her arms were so short. My dad was an engineer.

The only interesting thing my mother said was that she wanted me to meet some girl that was the friend or daughter or cousin of some acquaintance of hers. I called her back after I got off work.

"Why are you trying to set me up with girls?"

"I saw on your Facebook that Amanda broke up with you. Are you OK?"

I sighed. She would think that. I crossed the street to stop at the food trucks outside the NYU Stern building.

"First off, I broke up with her." I joined the line in front of the hibachi truck.

"It doesn't matter sweetie." She didn't believe me.

"I did, Mom, why don't you believe me?"

"Oh, of course I believe you. Why didn't you tell me?" It was my turn to order.

"Can I get the shrimp and fried rice?" I handed over a ten. The old Korean man nodded and began making my meal, the wrinkles around his eyes becoming more pronounced as he worked. I stared at his ear hair.

"I didn't tell you because I didn't want to have this conversation."

"What conversation?" She knew what I meant. She was going to make me say it.

"The one where you ask if I'm okay and refuse to accept that I'm fine."

"Are you OK?"

"Yes."

"Are you sure?"

"Yes." The vendor put my food in a Styrofoam container, which he placed in a plastic bag. He added a few napkins and a fork and passed it through the window of the black and red truck to me. I nodded in thanks and headed off to eat my food. I cracked open the container and scooped out a little brown rice and a piece of the succulent shrimp. Just as I spooned it into my mouth, my mother decided I wasn't going to say anything more and it was up to her to end the silence.

"It's just that... Zach," I could see her searching for the right words. She stood in the kitchen of her new house, but I pictured her in our old house, like how she used to stand when I was a little kid and I would come home from playing outside and I'd be all muddy and she'd be on the phone. She would just look at me and smile and hold up a finger to tell me, *wait*. She used to lean against the door frame and curl her finger around the cord of the phone. She still used phones with cords to this day because she couldn't understand how cordless ones worked. We had a bright red telephone that my dad brought home from some novelty shop. It had a rotary dial, that's how old it was.

"You always take breakups so hard. I don't want you to react like last time." She was referring to me crying after my ninth-grade girlfriend, Susan, broke up with me after three weeks. That was the last time I told my mother about any of my entanglements until Amanda insisted I change my relationship status.

"I'll be fine, Mom, really." What I didn't say was that my new strategy of coping was to get fucked up every time I thought of Amanda until the memory of proposing to her was completely erased due to alcohol and drug abuse.

"I have to go, Mom."

"Okay, sweetie. Call me soon, I want you to meet Zoey, I really think you'll like her."

"All right, Mom, fine." *Who knows?* I thought, *Maybe Zoey is the one.* A cynical smile crossed my face.

"I love you," she said. Every single phone conversation we've had since I was a freshman in college had ended like this one.

"Goodbye, Mom." I tapped end call. *Finally,* I thought, *Now I can eat.* I removed the Styrofoam container from the plastic bag and sat down. I had wandered without realizing it into the middle of Washington Square Park. It wasn't too cold, so I decided to stay. The trees were beginning to rebound from a harsh winter, and their variety of greens cheered me up. It never ceased to amaze me the effect simple colors can have on our brain chemistry and subsequently our moods.

I carried the container and the bag in each hand as I walked towards the fountain. It wasn't on, of course, and a group of kids were standing in the middle of it. A middle-aged woman was organizing them for a photo with the arch in the background. I walked around the opposite side so I was directly between the kids and the arch. I threw the plastic bag in a black metal trash can as I moved. I found a space in between two of the shorter kids where I could see the woman's camera. I heard her counting down to take the picture. I pulled my hood on with my left hand and put on the goofiest face I could while staring into the camera. The flash went off, and I moved on.

I sat down on one of the benches along the middle circle of the park, around the fountain. The difference between now and what it would be like in a few months was striking-- there were few kids, fewer colors, and the mood was more just one of persistence at getting through the day rather than hopefulness. I saw students rushing to class, businessmen talking loudly on their phones and none of the carefree people, of all ages, that fill the park when it's warm out.

I ate slowly, making up stories for the students as they passed. There goes a pre-med who just wants to be in Tisch but her parents won't let her. There goes a Sternie whose GPA has steadily dropped over the course of the semester and now he won't get a job while all his friends start working on Wall Street. Watch as he tries to hide the quiet desperation that has filled him since he realized one year, 3 months, two weeks and five days ago that he just wasn't good enough, no matter how hard he worked, to succeed in the field he had spent years and thousands of dollars in loans studying. It was the eyes. They could never hide the eyes. He dressed in the business casual of a Sternie, and he looked good. Maroon button-down with a black skinny tie, and black pants. Handsome, his shoulder-length black hair and strong jawline gave him the face needed to succeed in business. But his light brown eyes cried out as he walked by, revealing the shortcomings of the brain behind them. I surmised all this in between bites of shrimp and fried egg, in the five seconds it took him to walk across my field of vision. I did not turn my head to watch.

Bzzz. A text message. I removed my phone from my jeans and noticed a stain near the crotch. Damn. It looked like I might have to put on a new pair for the first time in a few days. *Yo wassup man?* It was Randy. *Eatin lunch.* Randy had graduated summa cum laude a year before me from CAS. That's the College of Arts and Sciences. He was unemployed. *Just picked up. You wanna swing by after work?* He spent his time getting high and yelling at his mom for yelling at him to get a job and move out. *Sure.*

I finished my shrimp and rice. I grabbed a few strands of rice and squeezed them together. I licked my fingers as I stood and threw out my container. The trash was full and I struggled to squeeze it in. As I walked away, a gust of wind blew the uppermost trash off the pile, including my container. Fuck. I ignored it. I pictured my dad lecturing me as he stuffed the trash down in the kitchen of our old home about being responsible. Then I went back and got my container and carried it to the next trash can.

* * *

When I got to Randy's mother's apartment, it was evident he had started without me. I had gotten off work later than usual. The walk to Randy's always took longer than it should too. I got so distracted. Randy lived out on Avenue C in Alphabet City. I walked down West 8th, and the transition from upper class Greenwich Village to run-down Avenue C always caught my eye. Each block was a step lower down the social ladder. As you went, the number of boarded-up buildings went up, and the number of white people went down.

I arrived at Randy's mother's dilapidated apartment building and pressed the button next to Amendola. I noticed the increase in graffiti since my last visit. FUCK IT, it said in curly black letters just to the left of the door. Under that was an unintelligible symbol presumably indicating authorship of the above. The buzzer rang. I pushed the door open and stepped over the broken vodka bottles in the entryway. A middle-aged black woman with wizened skin and thin curly hair dyed black looked me over. She turned away. She didn't dislike me, she felt no emotion towards me whatsoever. I climbed the three flights to Randy's tiny one bedroom, taking care to skip the step I knew our mutual friend Clyde had puked on recently.

Randy opened the door wearing athletic shorts and an open blue button-down over a beater. He was barefoot. A wave of smoke followed behind him. The smell hit me like a man finally giving in to temptation and beating his wife.

"Kev's already here." Randy smiled. I hadn't said anything funny, so I figured they'd been smoking for a while. The corners of his mouth poked out from beneath his bushy brown mustache, and he ran a hand through his greasy hair.

"How's the job hunt coming?" I walked past him and grabbed the joint he was holding. I placed it in my mouth and inhaled deeply. Pinching it between my teeth, I was able to continue smoking while removing my shoes and jacket.

"Fuck you," Randy said. I wasn't sure if he was referring to my question or my theft of his marijuana. I took the five steps through the kitchen and past the bathroom, barely looking at the mounting pile of dirty dishes stacked in the sink and general messiness of the apartment. "There's a lot of people out there looking for the Art History major that's going to put their company over the top." I turned to look at him. Five years ago, he had been on top of the world. His whole future ahead of him. So many paths to choose from. He had chosen badly, and all the potential in the world couldn't help him walk back the other way down that path and choose again. I finished the joint and threw it in the overflowing trash.

"That sucks, man, you know I'm just messin' around." I nodded towards the disgusting kitchen. "Devin leave again?"

"Quit calling her that."

"That's her name, ain't it?"

"She's my mom."

"You want me to call her Mrs. Amendola?" I smirked at him. He walked past me into the bedroom that was apparently now his.

"Whatever man, let's just get high." No argument from me. I followed Randy and his personal smoke cloud into the bedroom. Kevin sat on the bed, shoes off, head leaned back against the wall, eyes closed. I could barely see him from all the smoke. He was still wearing most of his suit from work, though the jacket was discarded over by the window, lying on the floor. I noticed the tiny wire pulled from the smoke detector above me. Randy joined Kevin on the bed, I took the only chair in the room, an old cushioned rocking chair, the color of which could only be described as burnt mustard. It had patches on it where Randy's cat Washington had scratched at it. Kevin passed Randy the blunt he was holding. He picked up a bong. I caught Randy's eye and looked at the vaporizer in the corner. He nodded.

Kevin started coughing. He put the bong down quickly. After a few moments, he took the blunt back from Randy, who picked up the bong. Kevin took a hit.

"So what happened with that Kate girl last night man?" His voice was lower than normal from the smoke. I packed the vape and answered without looking up.

"I got laid man. You?"

"Nah, she just wanted to fool around." Randy and Kevin laughed. I wasn't high yet.

"They were only freshman, you know that?" I looked up now. Kevin and Randy were each tugging on the bong. The blunt had gone out. I pulled open the dresser next to me and took out a pre-rolled joint. I tossed it on the bed. Randy won, and Kevin dejectedly picked up the joint.

"Yeah, I kind of figured when we went back to Hayden. The Miley Cyrus poster also gave me a clue." He looked around for a lighter, dramatically patting his t-shirt as if he had a breast pocket and then checking his back pockets. He knew he didn't have a lighter, he was just making it obvious he wanted one. I reached for my peacoat.

"That doesn't bother you? They said they were seniors." I unzipped the inside pocket of my coat and pulled out a condom and my Bic. I tossed the Bic to Kevin and put the condom back in the pocket. Kevin missed the lighter and it fell next to the bed.

"Nah, man. Look, you've been out of the scene for a while with Amanda. But that's just kind of the way it works." Kevin found the lighter and expertly lit up the joint. Randy coughed from behind the bong.

'What do you mean?" I noticed for the first time what was bugging me. It wasn't the cliche Bob Marley posters Randy had put up in Devin's absence, or the strikingly incongruous Van Gogh copy that he had hung up above the headboard. There was no music playing.

"Well as you--"

I cut Kevin off. "Randy can we play some tunes man? It's so quiet in here."

Randy jumped at his name. "Sure man, I just don't wanna be too loud, the landlord's been looking for rent and I don't have it." He got up off the bed and grabbed his MacBook. It was still covered in NYU-related stickers. Macklemore quietly filled the silence. Kevin looked vacant, but was alert enough to take advantage of Randy's absence and grab the bong. He passed the joint, which was down to a stub, to Randy as he sat back down.

"What were you sayin' Kev?" I wanted to hear this. I wanted as many girls as possible in the next few weeks. I needed to win this break-up, to show Amanda she should ask me to come back. I needed any advice I could get, even from Kevin, who could be kind of a creep when it came to women.

"I don't remember." Kevin looked at me. His eyes were bloodshot.

"It's simple, Zach." Randy cut in. He finished the joint and looked at me. I reached into the drawer and tossed him another. The vape had heated up, so I leaned down and took a deep, long hit. I looked back up. Randy was preparing for a speech. He always talked the most when we got high. Amanda frowned at me in my head and I felt a headache coming on. I took another hit. God, I wanted to be high.

"You, well, we, are getting older. The age of girls that are looking for one-night stands has remained the same as it was when we were freshman." Randy enunciated each word clearly. It was like he was back in college, serving as a TA and loving it. "The women that are our age are starting to look towards stage two, and they don't want a guy who will sleep with them and never call them." Kevin pulled at his tie in discomfort.

"Just take it off man," I said to him. He didn't respond. I took another hit of the vaporizer. And another. My chest started to feel warm. Ahhh.

"Kevin." He looked up. "Just take the tie off if it's so annoying."

"Ahhh, I would. I just always forget it when we leave."

"I'll remind you." I looked back to Randy. He appeared to have forgotten he was talking. He ran his hand through his hair. "What do you mean, stage two? What is that?" I took another hit of the vaporizer. I blew the vapor out towards the smoke detector and laughed.

Randy brightened. He had all these theories of life. I was sure this was another one, that he would describe passionately until he tripped again and came up with a new one. "It's my new theory. There are two stages to life, right? Potential and realization. We spend the first twenty-two years of our lives talking about potential." He stopped talking suddenly. He looked out the window. "Did you hear that?"

Kevin and I glanced at each other. "What?"

"I thought I heard the doorbell."

"You're getting paranoid, man," Kevin started making strange faces at Randy. "You scared of your landlord? Or your mommy?" Randy punched Kevin's arm. I took a hit. Kevin punched Randy's arm. I laughed. They both looked at me and started giggling. Randy stopped and got serious. A bead of sweat glistened as it slid from the side of his left eye down his scruffy cheek.

"So for two decades we have people helping us. Tryin' to get us to be our best, and helping us pick a career. We have so many options. Then we pick. That's the end of stage one."

"Okay…" I said, unsure of his point. "So what's stage two?" My phone vibrated. I pulled it out. It wasn't Amanda.

"Stage two is we get married and have kids and guide our kids through stage one. That's all there is to life. Our parents prepare us to get married and have kids and we prepare those kids to get married and have kids and they prepare those kids to get married and have kids and--"

"I get it," I cut in. Kevin giggled.

"Kids and parents, that's all we are." He pulled out his phone and looked at it. Kevin grabbed his phone and looked at it. Not wanting to be left out, I checked the message from earlier. *u comin to Louies thing tonigt?* It was Murph. Everyone needs a friend like Murph. If they're named Murph, that's even better. Murph makes it his mission to get all the old college boys together every couple of months or so. He only graduated last year, so he's still making the effort to keep in touch. I was like that last year, calling everyone up and having them over. Not this year though. I loved Murph. Louie too. Hell, I even loved stupid Kevin and smart-ass Randy.

"So basically, stage one is all excitement and possibilities." Randy continued. He looked at me sternly. "Stage two is realization of one of those possibilities, and normally includes the realization that you realized the wrong possibility." Kevin patted him on the back.

"C'mon, man, shit gets better." Eloquent as always.

"Then you force your kids through stage one and try to get them to do what you never did." Randy was killing the high.

"What are you guys doin' tonight?" I asked Kevin and Randy, eager to change the subject. They seemed confused.

"This." Randy had little desire to go out these days.

"You guys wanna hang with Louie and Murph?"

"Muuuurph," Kevin said, laughing. "Of course, I love Murph."

"Hell yeah man, when we goin'?" Randy said. We all giggled. I turned off the vape and gestured for the bong. Randy passed it over happily. Kevin gave me my lighter back. I took a hit. Kevin and Randy started arguing about the Yankee's chances this season. I had no interest, and my mind wandered…

I slammed the door to our apartment as Amanda and I came in. It was a Saturday, towards the end of our senior year at NYU. "Zach?" I heard Brian call out weakly from his room. "Is that you?"

"Yeah," I called back. I scanned the mess. No food left out, that was good. Both Kevin and Murph's doors were half-open in a way that suggested they had gone out.

"Come in here man." I looked at Amanda, her smile as she surveyed the apartment the same as it always was. I jerked my head to tell her to follow me, and made my way to Brian's room. I stepped over someone's dirty jeans and put a hand on the door, which was slightly ajar. I stepped inside.

Brian was lying on the bed, wearing athletic shorts and a white v-neck, which he was holding onto with both hands. Most of his belly was showing. He smiled at me lazily. I turned around and stopped Amanda from following me in.

"You wanna do something later?" I asked her. She tried to peer past me. I shifted with her.

"Suuuure," she said slowly. "I thought we were going to hang out now?" She brushed her hair out of her eyes.

"I remembered I have to do something. For class." I noticed the bag of shrooms lying on Brian's desk, just out of Amanda's view. There was still about half an eighth left, I guessed.

"Um, okay, I guess. Text me?" Amanda clearly didn't believe me. But she left. As soon as I heard the door shut, I started eating the shrooms. They tasted dirty.

"Hurry up man," Brian said from somewhere behind me. "I'm an hour in. They are… potent."

"Patience is a virtue," I said between mouthfuls. I went to the kitchen and drank some water to wash them down. I returned to Brian's room and sat on the chair by his desk.

Twenty minutes later, they started hitting.

Forty minutes later, Brian and I had started talking.

An hour later, we were bouncing off the walls.

We would talk about something so passionately, debating and agreeing for ten or fifteen minutes, then reach some satisfying conclusion. Thirty seconds later, we had no recollection of what we had been talking about. I only remember one conversation from that trip.

I got a text from Kevin. There was some frat party that night that he wanted to go to.

"You wanna go to a frat thing?" Brian looked up from the bed spread he had been thoroughly examining.

"Not really," he said. "Watching jocks who wish they hadn't come here hit on girls who aren't smart enough to be here?" He stopped abruptly and looked around. "Actually, I'm in. I think in this state of mind I just might be able to deal with the amount of testosterone in the room."

I texted Kevin asking why we were going to a frat party. He shot back quickly that a bunch of the girls from our sophomore floor, Six East, were going.

"Ah," I said to no one. "A reunion." I directed my words to Brian. "It's a Six East event." He laughed. I texted back that Brian and I would go.

"I don't like this whole community thing we have going on," Brian said. He sat up. I felt the air in the room shift. We had reached an important topic, something worth discussing in great detail for at least ten minutes.

"Whaddyou mean?" I scratched my chest. I felt grimy, like I always did towards the end of the trip.

"I feel like everyone thinks we all stick together because we lived on the same floor and had this great big community." Brian looked at me. His cheeks were red.

"Yeah, but really, I'm just friends with some of the kids that lived on that floor," I agreed, as I was obligated to do. We had long ago laid down ground rules for these trips: It was a safe space where we could say anything, no matter how crazy it sounded, and the other would either agree or just listen. It was part of the reason I liked tripping with Brian, but not with my other friends, who I always felt were restrained with me, or were judging me when I said crazy things.

"Exactly. I don't give a fuck about Six East." Brian scratched his chin. I ground my teeth. They felt weird. I looked around for a piece of chewing gum. "Here," Brian said. He tossed me a piece.

"Like, I'm not going to hang out with these kids after we graduate." I unwrapped the gum and slid it into my mouth.

"Well, I might, but it won't be out of any real kinship." I chewed as I thought this over. It sounded kind of like a disagreement. When I didn't respond, Brian continued. "I mean, I'll hang out with Murph and Kevin and Randy, but not because we lived on a floor together."

"Because we're actually friends." My voice rose as I finished the statement. I wasn't actually sure what he was getting at.

"Sure, in some sense. But we're only friends because we are similarly aged men who do similar things on the weekends. Not like…" He trailed off.

"Us?" I asked. We had never really discussed our relationship. He was my best friend. Hell, I loved him. But I would never say it.

"Yeah, I guess. Basically, what this boils down to, is you and I, we're best friends. Zach, you're my best friend." He looked away. I did too.

"Right." I laughed. "It took almost four years and a lot of drugs, but we can finally say it. You're my best friend." We were both uncomfortable.

"And with these other guys, I just feel like, we have so little in common. I mean, our friendships are so superficial. What do you really know about Kevin?" I considered the question. I knew biographical stuff, sure, and some of the things he liked, mainly his sexual preferences. But did I know him like I knew Brian? I didn't.

"I guess that's just how it works, though, isn't it?" I gained confidence in what I was saying as I spoke, mainly because I was just repeating what Brian had said. "Men, and I'd guess women, have only one or two truly close friends, and everyone else is just kind of out of… convenience." I took out my phone and considered writing this down.

"Yeah, and so we hang out, or hung out, with Six East, because they lived on our floor and they were kinda like us." He lay back against the wall, looking at me again.

"But aren't we like that? We were friends because we were roommates." I knew what he was going to say before he even opened his mouth. He spoke quietly.

"At first, of course. But I think we've changed. This boils down to, you and I are friends. And that's all we've really decided here."

"Great. Now I've gotta take a leak." I got up and walked towards the door.

"Zach?" I turned. Brian looked hyper vulnerable, his eyes were wide and he leaned towards me as he spoke. "I love you." We looked at each other, then both collapsed in a fit of laughter.

Kevin and Randy had finally agreed that the Yankees were pretty good. I looked at both of them. Not much had changed in the two years since we graduated. We hung out, but it was mainly to avoid making new friends. I didn't know much about them, and frankly I didn't have much interest in learning about them. It was kind of sad. I missed what I had with Brian, what I had with Amanda. I rolled another joint and lit it, smoking it to the very end.

* * *

We left sometime later, I'm not sure how long it was. I was high, but nowhere near as high as Kevin and Randy. We walked to West 4th street to take the subway into Brooklyn. *I wonder if Amanda will be there*, I thought. I resisted the urge to text her. I tuned in to what Kevin was saying as we walked.

"So basically, the computer buys it, and sells it a fraction of a second later. And if we do it with enough money, we make shit-tons without doing anything."

"That's sick man." Randy was watching the dog walking in front of us intently. The dog's owner, a middle-aged soccer mom with wavy black hair and a large wart under her right nostril, eyed him suspiciously.

"I get paid to just sit there and count how much money we are making." I laughed at that, and Kevin laughed, and Randy snickered. We passed a policeman standing on the corner, and he looked at us. We all shushed each other.

It started to drizzle just as we got to West 4th. We walked down the stairs, which were covered in tobacco stains and chewing gum. I avoided touching the handrails. Kevin and Randy slid their cards and went through the turnstiles. I couldn't get mine to work. After it had said "Swipe again at this turnstile" for the fifth time. I looked left and then jumped it. Or tried to. I tripped and landed almost head-first on the dirty ground. Kevin and Randy laughed. I cursed. My hands were disgusting. I wiped them on Randy. He hit me. I had an idea. I went over to the Indian man running the little store they had there and bought a People magazine. Kim and Kanye were on the cover. I wiped my hands on Kim's boobies. We laughed.

The A train pulled up. We piled on. Randy and I sat down. There was an old black man sitting next to me. He sniffed me. I recoiled. He smiled at me. He had all of his teeth, but they were as crooked as Nixon. "I'd like some of that," he said.

"*No hablo ingles.*" I shrugged my shoulders sorry at him. I turned to Kevin, who was trying to stand without holding on. He wasn't wearing his tie. I laughed at him. He looked at me with blood-shot eyes and raised one bushy eyebrow. I didn't explain. The train started, and Kevin fell. Randy, me, and the old black man all laughed heartily. A blond woman and her mixed-race daughter with braids got up and moved farther down the car.

We got off the subway at Atlantic Ave. I realized that I didn't remember where Louie lived in Brooklyn. I called him for directions. After a confusing half hour or so that involved a near-altercation with a homeless gentleman, we arrived at Louie's apartment in Williamsburg.

A girl I had never met opened the door. She was tall, almost my height (Six feet, or close enough). She had on a Harvard sweatshirt

and tight black jeans. The apartment was surprisingly large, and deco-
rated with all sorts of eastern stuff. I couldn't process it, there were
swords and robes and kimono dragons.

"Hi," the mystery girl said. Or I should say sang, maybe. Her
voice was lyrical. "I'm Erica. You friends of Greg's?" Her intonation
rose and fell as she sang. I loved it immediately.

"Well hello, madam, I am Zacharias Henry Johnston the third."
I bowed and offered her my hand. Kevin pushed past me. Randy was
preoccupied with the doorknob.

"You both talk funny," Kevin said. "And his name's actually Zachary," he added to the princess. I nodded. She laughed.

"You wanna drink?" She offered me a bottle. I grabbed at it eagerly.
"Woah, settle down." I laughed. Then I saw the label. Everclear.

"Oh boy," I said. "Somebody made a run to Jersey." I looked for
a mixer, but found only Hawaiian Punch.

"What do you mean?" She asked. I noticed she was swaying a
little bit.

"Everclear's illegal in New York." I poured both drinks at once
into a red solo cup I found. I had a flashback to freshman year…

"What is it?" I asked Brian. He laughed and leaned back in his
chair. We were sitting in our dorm room, him and me and two girls
who are no longer important. His shirt was unbuttoned, revealing his
toned and tanned six-pack beneath. He smiled at the girls, showing
them his white-teeth, before explaining to me: "It's Everclear, it's 95
percent alcohol." I remembered marveling at the business model of
watering down rubbing alcohol and selling it at fifty times the price.
Brian took a swig and I took one too. It burned on the way down, and
left a stinging sensation in the roof of my mouth. But Brian smiled so
I smiled. He winked at me.

"Are you going to drink that?" Erica looked at me like I was wearing
a tinfoil hat and complaining about the government stealing my mind-
waves. I realized I was just holding the cup. I tossed some of it back.

"You don't need to worry about me drinking…" I said.

"Good." she giggled and looked at me sideways. I felt like I had
known her my whole life.

A few drinks later, she was sitting on my lap. I still hadn't seen Louie. I began to wonder if we were at the wrong party. I looked for Kevin and Randy. Randy was examining the doorknob. I heard a yell from another room that sounded like Kevin. I was going to investigate, but Erica chose that moment to shove her tongue in my mouth. I kissed her back harder. She grabbed my hair. I hate that. Why do girls think I'll like that? It just causes me pain. Amanda never did that. She told me once, "The golden rule of sex is don't pull or insert anything without asking." I laughed into Erica's mouth. She pulled back.

"What's so funny?" She asked. I noticed she didn't seem as drunk as I was.

"Nothing," I said. I took a swig of the drink I was holding. It was empty. I threw it on the ground. The place had emptied out. My phone was vibrating. I ignored it. "Come here." I grabbed the back of her head and kissed her forcefully. I pulled her hair. She moaned. I guess some people like it.

I opened my eyes. Her's were closed. *Why do we close our eyes to kiss?* I wondered. Does it have something to do with the shame our society has made us feel for having sex? We're taught from an early age that sex is dirty and that we should avoid it because girls will get pregnant and boys will get STD's and have to have their dicks cut off. So is the closing of our eyes an extension of that? Are we so ashamed we try not to look at our partner? Why am I not high? Am I drunk?

I noticed a freckle between her brows that I hadn't seen before. I fumbled with her bra strap. She pushed me away. I came back and we kissed again. I played with her nipple through her bra and shirt. I noticed a woman take a picture of us. She moaned. I hardened. She straddled me.

"Wait," I gasped. "We can't do this here."

"Why not?" she kissed me.

"You wanna go into the bedroom?" I spoke without disengaging our lips. To punctuate the request, I squeezed her boob.

"Okay," she breathed. I felt her hot breath on my neck and smelled the Everclear. We got up as one and walked to the bedroom, our fingers intertwined. I stepped over a dark figure and almost tripped. *I guess I'm drunk,* I thought. As we approached, the door swung open. Two guys came out holding hands. I didn't know which one to high-five or bro-nod to. We slipped past them and the bulkier one nodded at me, so I figured he was the dominant one and nodded at him. But the other one, who wore a large cross around his neck and was shirt-less, dapped me up as we passed. Very confusing.

We stepped through the doorframe. To my right was a dresser with a half empty bottle of Captain Morgan's on it, next to a hairbrush that had several long blond hairs in it. I grabbed the bottle. Erica went and sat on the bed. I unscrewed the top and threw it against the wall. She removed her shoes, then her pants.

"Take off your socks," I commanded.

"Whoopsies, I didn't notice." she removed the articles and we giggled. She reached out to me. I gulped down some rum and spilled some on the ground.

"Youno whatI liketodo whenI'mdrunk," I slurred.

"What?" I sat down on the bed next to her and kissed her neck. I took off her shirt and kissed down between her cleavage. I stopped and took another swig.

"Go downtown." I kissed her belly button. I tried to take off her bra and failed. She removed it with one hand. She kissed my hair and pulled it. Ugh. She leaned in.

"I'll be right back," she whispered.

"Ah," I said. "The mysterious pre-coitus visit to the facilities. Make haste, my darling, I yearn for your flesh." She ignored me and went into the bathroom. I wondered what girls do in there when they leave right before sex. Put out a welcome mat? Comb? My head drooped to the ground.

A wedding. But whose? I see all the groomsmen. Kevin and Randy and Murph. Oh, it must be Brian's. Where is he though? Is he in the bathroom? And who is he marrying? I see Amanda and my mother looking at me. I go over to talk to them. But I don't get near them. They keep pointing towards the front.

"Are you ready to go downtown? Zach?" Erica was back from her venture to the other side of the plaster. I awoke with a start.

"Being a God-kissing carrion." I knocked on the headboard and placed my ear up to it. I looked at Erica. "Yep, I'm drunk." She looked so beautiful. I had to have her. I grabbed her and threw her on the bed. She giggled. I took off her panties and buried my face between her legs. She moaned with delight. I thought about how silly it is that we drive on a parkway and park on a driveway. I wondered what Kevin was doing. I thought about the Jolly Rancher story that people always talked about on reddit. I hoped it wasn't true. I felt my eyes grow heavy.

Wait. I realize it can't be Brian's wedding. He'd never get married. He always told me that. "Why limit myself?" he'd say. I realize in this instance that it was fear, not bravado, that made him say that. A second later the thought is gone, it slips between my fingers without a sound. So whose wedding am I floating at? Because I am floating, I notice. I am above all the other guests. An invisible hand, like Adam Smith prophesied, delivers me to the stage. It is my wedding, I surmise. A unicorn runs past. I giggle. Then I start to freak out. Who am I marrying? Music starts playing. It's "Black Magic Woman" by Santana. I never got why they are called Santana when he doesn't even sing. I turn, and a woman is walking down the aisle. Is this my wife? She is so beautiful. She turns and sits down. I reach for my lighter and a cigarette and pull out a carton of silly string. My hands start to melt. A woman wearing a wedding dress and a veil walks down the aisle. A Mexican Mariachi band starts playing. All of the band members have facial hair that goes from ear to ear, but skips the chin and goes over the mouth instead. "Here comes the bride," I sing. "Who will she be?"

"Zach?" Erica's voice startled me. I awoke with my face still in her nether regions. *Never woken up in one of these before*, drunken me thought.

"Well, not for a long time anyway." I said.

"What?"

"Huh?"

"Are you too drunk for this?"

"Of cour not. Where a condom?" I kiss my way back up to her lips. I was naked. Huh. That was new. I saw a condom and put it on. At first I tried the wrong way, but I got it eventually.

"Maybe we shouldn't do this."

"How old are you?"

"What? I'm 21."

"Hmmm. So you are a stage one. I think I am a stage one still as well. But maybe not."

"What are you talking about?"

"Looking for love in all the wrong places." My singing was off-key. Strange, I was normally a good singer.

"Look, this was a mistake. We are too drunk for this. I should go."

"Okly dokles. Look both ways before you cross the street, Erica. You little cutie you." Erica stands up and gets dressed. I stare at her left butt cheek. Why does such a shape arouse me? It causes a certain set of neurons to fire, which causes other circuits of neurons to fire, which eventually sends a signal down to increase blood flow. Funny, the way evolution prepared me to attempt to drunkenly hook up with a stranger in a two-bedroom brownstone in Williamsburg. Erica put on her necklace.

"I'm going to leave now, okay?" She stood in the doorway.

"I think I'm at the wrong party…" I moaned. She left. I passed out.

We are off on our honeymoon. Wait, what about the wedding? I can't see her face. Every time I turn towards her, she is looking away. She has dirty blond hair and a mole on the left side of her neck. That's all I know. She doesn't do it on purpose. I look at her and she is looking out at the water. I look at her and she looks for a waiter to order. I look at her and she dives into the pool.

We live out our life. I never see her face. We raise two beautiful children and I never see their faces either. All of this happens so fast. Then, I am somewhere different. The smell of freshly mown grass overwhelms me. I am lying in a graveyard. I get up. I see a tombstone. "Alex Foster, born 1924, died 1938." A part of me cries for this forgotten stranger, who lived fourteen years and will never think again. The amount of energy that went into creating him is overwhelming. And it was all for nothing. He never left stage one. But why am I here? I see a mass of people and walk over. My feet don't touch the ground.

She is dead. She lies in the coffin. I beg for them to open it, to let me see her face once. They think I mean one last time, I mean for the first time, let me see the woman I married. My children hold me back. I look at them and they turn to their wives. Their identical, cookie cutter wives with long brown hair and wonderful bosoms. Each has a single tear run down their cheek. I scream and yell and cry and they take me away.

Chapter 4

I woke up and looked at my phone. 4:27. I didn't know where I was. The smell of puke filled my nostrils. The recognition it was mine sent me running to the bathroom. I didn't make. *Fuck it, this isn't my apartment.* I threw up on the floor. I lay down and curled up into a ball. *I'm never drinking again.* I just wanted to pass out and wake up the next morning. The room was spinning. I squeezed my eyes shut. I put my hands over my eyes. I moaned. "Fuuuuck." I fell back asleep. I didn't dream, for once.

I was woken by a surfer-looking dude the next morning. He had spiky blond hair and a long face. He was frowning at me as he shook me awake with his right hand on my right shoulder.

"Who are you, man?"

An excellent question, though I believed he meant it in a more of a logistical sense than an existential one. I, however, was still a little buzzed from the night before.

"Who are any of us?" I sat up and found I was clutching a pillow. It was puke colored with puke colored stains.

"Oh, great man. C'mon. What's your name?" Spiky was annoyed. I wasn't feeling too great myself.

"Listen, brah, I really better be going." A little man had started to pound his hands against the inside of my skull.

"Alright asshole, I was just going to kick you out. You could at least give me some money to pay to clean all this shit." Now he was getting aggressive. Jeez, some people. I sighed. He had a point, no matter how much of a douchebag he was being about it. The little man had switched to some sharp object, it felt more like a fork than a knife, that he was digging into my temple.

"Fine." His deep v was both too deep and too tight. I could see his nipples.

"Your shirt is pretty tight." I stood up and took out my wallet.

"Oh, is it, stranger I found passed out in my bedroom?" I tossed a twenty on the bed.

"I'll be going now." I moved past him and he shouldered me a little bit. I would have retaliated, but he got a little puke on him from my shirt, which he hadn't noticed. *Karma's a bitch*, I thought. I tapped my pockets to make sure I had my phone, wallet, and keys. I did. I nodded at Spiky, who glowered at me. The little man had recruited his children, who were stomping around on the edges of my brain.

Outside, I noticed that the horrible smell of the apartment had followed me. Intuitively, I figured it was actually me that smelled, specifically the puke covering all my clothes. I didn't want to ride the subway back looking like a homeless man, so I called Louie. I figured he must live nearby, as I was supposed to be there the night before.

"What's up, man? Where were you last night?"

"Sorry man, we were so high we went to the wrong party."

"Oh, that's crazy." I turned left and hoped I was walking in the right direction.

"Yeah, I had a pretty crazy night. I got mad cross-faded and passed out in some surfer-dude's bedroom."

"That sucks man. You should have been here."

"Yeah. Listen man, I'm a mess. Can I swing by and shower before I go back uptown?"

"Oh, ah, sure. You know where I live? Gonna find me this time?"

I chuckled. So did the little man, which made my head hurt. He gave me directions. I was pretty close. He lived in a brownstone just a few blocks away. I got there in no time. I pressed the buzzer. It was obvious he had just moved in, the line where his name was written had another name that was crossed out. It said, "~~Anderson~~ Reynolds. 5b." Most of the other apartments were vacant. Or at least they didn't have names listed.

Louie buzzed me up. The place was a complete mess. Boxes were strewn everywhere, the kitchen counter was covered with empty bottles, the sight of which caused my stomach to lurch, and there was a faint aroma of puke. Oh no, wait, that was still me. Louie came forward to greet me, then stopped short at the sight of me. There was a full-length mirror lying against a pile of boxes marked "Clothes and shit." I looked, and regretted it. My shirt, once white, was a pinkish-orange in spots and a brownish-yellow in others. My jeans were torn at each knee, and they seemed darker in spots jeans shouldn't be darker.

"Here." Louie had grabbed a trash bag and offered it to me. "Why don't you just throw those out? You can wear some of my clothes."

"Can I?" Louie was a good five or six inches shorter than me, and probably twenty or thirty pounds heavier. I regretted the remark as soon as I said it. Louie's face darkened. I could see the gears turning as he tried to decide how to interpret my response. I did my best to arrange my face into what I hoped was "grateful." Apparently I was successful, because he cracked a smile.

"Of course man, I'll always help out an old Six-Easter." He was referring to the floor we had all lived on our Sophomore year. Sometimes it seemed like I didn't have any friends that didn't go to NYU. I thanked him profusely and stripped. I dumped the shirt and the jeans in the bag.

"Bathroom's that way."

"Thanks."

"Here, you can use…" he looked around, walked over to the mirror, and grabbed an Anakin Skywalker towel from the boxes marked "Clothes and shit." He tossed me the towel. I caught it and slung it over my shoulder. Louie eyed my dollar-sign boxers. I walked away to the bathroom.

As the water washed over me, I examined the blue-green tiles beneath my feet and felt sober enough to reflect on the last night. In all likelihood, I figured, I had simply added another member to my Never Contact Contacts list. Basically, anytime I got too drunk and hooked up with some girl but didn't sleep with her, I would normally wake up the next day to find she had given me her number in the hopes I would call her and we would date. I have never ever contacted one of these girls. I just wouldn't know what to say. "Hi, we made out last night and I'm pretty sure your name is Francine, want to come over and fuck tonight?"

I examined Louie's shampoo selection, of which there were a surprising number of them. I just had shampoo and conditioner, but Louie had all different scents and effects. I selected Aquatic Breeze and sudsed up my hair. It was getting a little long. I was approaching the point of no return, where I'd have to cut it or invest in a comb.

Louie was waiting for me when I got out of the shower. He had picked out some sweatpants and his stretchiest t-shirt for me to wear. I dried my hair.

"I don't have any food, but we could go to a diner or something if you want."

"Nah, I just want to get back and lie down." I dropped the towel and put on the pants.

"Oh, well. It would be good to catch up sometime, it's been a while." Louie picked up the towel. I felt bad.

"You don't have to pick up after me, I was just leaving it there for a second."

"It's totally fine man. You're my guest." I put on the shirt. It was loose in the chest but did not quite reach my waist. I pulled the cord on the sweatpants as far as I could. They almost reached my ankles.

"Well. Thanks. And we should catch up sometime. Just not when I'm insanely hungover." I grabbed my phone and wallet and keys and slipped them into the pockets of the sweatpants. I checked my phone. One missed call.

"What are you doing tonight?"

"Huh? Uh, I don't know yet." I looked up.

"Well me and Kevin were going to pick up some brownies. From California. If you wanna join us you could contribute right now…"

Hmmm. Edibles. Well, they would keep me from drinking. I'd be too fucked up to want alcohol. "Yeah, that sounds good." I threw him a twenty. "When did you see Kevin?"

"He came to the party last night. Said you hooked up with some hot girl." He handed me a ten back. Cool. Cheap edibles. My favorite kind.

"Yeah, I guess I did." I headed for the door, bracing myself for the cold walk to the subway. "Text me tonight."

"Peace bro."

"Goodbye Louie."

I took out my phone and saw that I had never checked the missed call. My heart skipped a beat. It was Amanda. I wanted to call her, but I was at the subway station. I texted her: "Bout to b on the subway. Wats up?" I pressed send and shook my head sorry to the homeless man sitting on the stairs. He nodded in response and wrapped his brown blankets tighter around himself. I shivered.

When I got off the train I had a text from Amanda asking me to call her when I could. So I did. It's… interesting how easily I follow her directions. She asked to meet me for lunch tomorrow. She didn't sound happy or sad. I wasn't sure how I should feel either. Lunch certainly isn't a "I want to get back together and spend all night having make-up sex" kind of event, but it's also not a "please don't be at your place at this time so I can get my stuff" thing either.

* * *

Louie texted me around 9 telling me to come over. I had forgotten about the edibles. I was still recovering from the night before, drinking cup after cup of water and sitting absentmindedly in front of the TV. But I did want to see him, to reminisce. So I put on my most comfortable jeans and a purple polo I had recently bought that was the softest thing I had ever worn. I was about to leave when I remembered I had a stress ball I had gotten at some work event a few weeks back. I dug around under a pile of dirty clothes I had lying next to my bed for the sweatshirt I had worn to that event. I hadn't worn it since because I caught a glimpse of myself in a mirror there, and before my brain recognized me, it said, *that is an ugly sweatshirt.* I've always found it hard to accurately appraise my looks. Context clues have told me I'm good-looking, but I don't see it. I look in the mirror and all I see are flaws. My nose is crooked, my skin is blemished and pale, and if you look closely you can see the tiny hairs between my eyebrows form a unibrow. I've found the only time I can accurately tell how good I look is when I see myself in a mirror when I'm not expecting to, and my subconscious evaluates me just like it would any other person, with none of the esteem-protectors it has built-in when I look in a mirror. And I normally like what I see. But this sweatshirt made me look creepy.

I found the sweatshirt under a neon t-shirt that a coworker gave me and that I had worn once so that he wouldn't think I didn't like it. The stress ball was in the pocket. I transferred it to my back pocket. I also grabbed a bag of low-calorie rice cakes for when I got the munchies. I headed out the door and reversed the path I took that morning. The sky was a hazy blue. It never really got black here. Too many lights. I read a study once that said if you judged city limits by luminance, the borders of New York City stretch from D.C to Boston. So I guess I didn't really move away when I went to college, I just moved to a different part of the city. I bounced the ball once on the ground and regretted it. I considered washing my hands. Then I decided I'm 24 years old and I'm not going to be intimidated by the filthiness of these streets. I had lived here for six years. A siren went off in the distance and I jumped. A little black boy walking past with his mother laughed and pointed at me. I glared at him and his faux Timberlands clomping on the sidewalk.

"Excuse me." My words stopped the woman in her tracks. She eyed me suspiciously, then softened. There was that effect. I smiled at her. The boy frowned.

"Yes?"

"You wouldn't happen to have any raisins, would you?" I'm normally staunchly against pick-up lines. But in situations like this I don't have much of a choice. I can't just strike up a normal conversation like we're at a bar. So when I do have to use a line, I go corny. And I mean really, really corny.

"No…" She's intrigued, but also put off. I noted the hastily applied makeup, the loose sweatshirt and the functional flats on her feet. She was a single mom. She didn't have time to worry about what men out on the streets think of her. But she was also… voluptuous. She hadn't walked away yet. It's times like these where I think I must be attractive to women. If I was ugly, they would leave when I started acting weird, instead of finding it cute or even endearing.

"How about a date, then?" The wheels turned in her head. I watched with a bright smile. Junior scowled at me. She got it. She laughed, way more than the pun deserved. I won.

"Okay, well, that's unique. Sure, I guess. Let me give you my number." My phone was already out. She told me the number and I faithfully tapped it in. I looked at Junior, he had crossed the arms of his mini peacoat and was watching the interaction with disgust.

"And your name?"

"Grace."

* * *

I buzzed up to Louie's unsure of what the scene would be. I hadn't done edibles in a while, and I hadn't done edibles with Louie in even longer. Kevin was already there. He'd dressed down, for once. His Saturday attire still involved a button-down, and today's version was a sleek black with white buttons, but he was wearing jeans and the button-down was untucked.

"The fuck are those shoes, man?" I said. He was defensive. Maybe this was why he always wore loafers.

"They're my new vans. You like 'em?" He flexed each ankle to show off his new shoes-- a pair of bright pink canvas sneakers that screamed Flamboyant Gay Man.

"I love 'em. Where can I get a pair?" He thought I was being sarcastic, but I supported anything that made him look like more of an asshole. I found it amusing.

"Louie went out to pick up, he'll be back in a bit." Kevin walked into the kitchen and I followed him.

"Cool." I opened the refrigerator.

"When's the last time you ate?" Kevin looked at me, serious.

"A few hours ago, why?" I closed the fridge and grabbed an apple from the handmade fruit basket on the granite counter next to the silver oven-grill combo.

"You should probably eat something. These things will really fuck you up on an empty stomach." I put the apple back.

"Good," I said. I walked out of the kitchen.

"I'm serious," Kevin called after me. He followed me into the main room. I plopped down on Louie's beige pleather couch. I kicked off my shoes and placed my feet on the glass coffee table.

"Pretty impressive furniture for a… what is Louie doing these days?" Kevin looked shocked at how comfortable I was. He hated relaxing sober. He also didn't appreciate the change of subject. He sat on the recliner adjacent to the couch and turned it to face me. After a few seconds, he reluctantly answered.

"He's a writer."

"Still pursuing that? What's he been in?" I picked up a magazine off the coffee table and flipped through it.

"Nothing that I know of."

"Kim hates being pregnant… surprising. So then how's he paying for this?" I managed to tear my eyes away from the cover story to look at Kevin. I could guess how he was paying for it, I just wanted to see if Kevin could confirm it. He nodded.

"You know," he said.

"Ah," I said. We sat in silence for a few minutes. I learned more about Kim Kardashian than I wanted to know.

"Look," he began. I snapped out of my fantasy about a butt implant gone horribly wrong. She probably wouldn't die anyways. "I know that the last month and a half has been tough for you. It's been hard for me too."

"Oh boy! An inspiring speech about dealing with grief!" I clapped my hands and bounced up and down.

"Amanda breaking up with you on top of Brian's death. It's a miracle you're still working." He nervously met my eyes to gauge my reaction. It wasn't good. I clenched my jaw. Kevin was my second best friend. Or, he was my new best friend. I'd let him finish.

"But I think you are not dealing with this the right way. And maybe I'm not either. We've been getting fucked up. And I know we always get fucked up. But we've been getting really fucked up, especially the last few nights. We spent hours at some drug dealer we didn't know's party last night, Zach."

"I'd been meaning to ask, when did you leave that? I didn't make it out till morning." I laughed. Kevin didn't. He looked up and met my eyes. There was water clouding his dark eyes. He scratched behind his left ear, and I noticed a patch of skin in his crew cut.

"Stop changing the subject. I know it hurts. But drugging yourself up isn't the answer." His face changed abruptly. He seemed to have just realized this himself.

"Then why are you here?" I had caught him being a hypocrite. He had no choice but to change the subject.

"You're right." He stood up. He walked over to the coat rack and grabbed his jacket.

"You're leaving?" I got up and walked over to him. This was not what I thought was going to happen.

"Yes, and you should too. We don't need to do this. Let's take a night off from the drugs and the women. Let's talk about Brian, about what happened to him." I opened the door for him.

"See you around." I refused to look at him, focusing out the door. Louie appeared in the doorway. He was disheveled and his hair was wet.

"Jesus, it's pouring out there. Where you guys goin'?" Louie marched in without an answer and pulled out three purple packages. He placed them on the kitchen counter and looked at Kevin, then me.

"We're leaving." Kevin looked at me.

"Kevin doesn't want his cookie. Here, I'll have it." I handed ten dollars to Kevin without making eye contact. He stared at it, then took it and nodded goodbye to Louie. I shut the door behind him. Louie asked me with a look for an explanation. I just shrugged my shoulders.

"Forget him. We're gonna have a good night," I said. I returned to the couch and sat back down.

"Feet off the table please."

"You can't be serious."

"'fraid so. I can't have you dirtying up the place. Bad for business." He sat down in the recliner and pulled the lever to lie down.

"You sell pot. You think anyone cares?" I took my feet off the table. I got up and grabbed two of the packages. "Jesus, these things have nutritional info?"

"Yep, they're legit." Louie smiled. He walked over and grabbed his. He had missed a spot whenever he most recently shaved, and there were a few hairs on his right cheek.

"Regular smokers of cannabis should consume 1/2 a cookie," I read aloud from the back. I opened the package and wolfed down the whole thing.

"Woah," Louie said. He chewed slowly on his. I remembered a meal I had with Brian a few months ago…

"You take forever," I said. Amanda and I were waiting for Brian to finish. Haley, his latest girl, his last girl, was in the bathroom. "Why can't you just eat at a normal speed like everyone else?" Amanda chuckled. She reached for my hand and smiled at me. She was wearing a black dress and the necklace I had bought her for her birthday a few weeks before. The light caught the emerald around her neck and for a second, she sparkled. Brian finished chewing, looking at Amanda the whole time. He swallowed. He looked at me.

"I'm sorry Zach, I know you do everything quickly. I like to take my time." Amanda laughed. I chuckled politely.

"Is that why it always takes us so long to leave when you just have to 'run to the bathroom' before we go?" Amanda guffawed. Brian had no response. It was the last time the three of us ate together.

"What do you want to do?" Louie asked after he finished his cookie. I opened the other cookie and ate it.

"Let's go sit somewhere where we can reminisce." I knew where we were going to go. I didn't want to have to dictate, so I tried to guide Louie to it.

"I got an idea, why don't we go sit at Brad's? For old times' sakes?" Bingo.

"I don't know, you sure you wanna?" I was just messing with him now. I imagined I was starting to feel it. I knew that it took an hour or so, but I always had a giddy effect right after eating something like this. The anticipation of it almost made me high.

"Yeah, let's do it." Louie giggled.

"Okay," I said. I put my shoes on slowly. "We could even call Murph and Randy to meet us there."

"Sounds good man." I got my coat.

We got there really early, around ten or so. I hadn't started to feel it yet. We got a table. There was almost no one there. I got a cranberry juice from the cute bartender.

"What're you on your period or something?" she asked, with a too-strong-to-be-real Boston accent. I laughed at the reference.

"Are you a cawp?" I mimed smashing my glass and hitting her with it. She smiled. "Isabel," her name tag read.

"Great movie," she said. I agreed. She was wearing an engagement ring.

"When's the big day?"

"A few months."

"You love him?" she seemed taken aback.

"Of course." How lucky she was. And she didn't even know it.

"Congratulations," I said. I tried to keep the bitterness out of my voice, but from her frown it was clear I failed. I walked back to Louie.

"Randy'll be here in a few. Murph's gonna meet us later. He's out to dinner with Jackie." I sat down next to Louie. We had our backs to the wall. This would be our entertainment for the evening.

"How's that going for him?" I took the stress ball out of my pocket and squeezed it a few times. Louie watched me play with it.

"Good, I think. They're getting pretty serious." I bounced the ball off the wall and caught it.

"How long has it been now?"

"Almost eight months, I think."

"I meant since we ate them."

"Oh." He checked his watch. He was the only guy our age I knew who wore a watch. It wasn't even a nice one either. It was one of those velcro watches that aren't water proof but are "water-resistant,' whatever that means. He wore this green and grey thing on his right wrist too, even though he was right-handed. "It's 10:17." He looked at me. "When did we take them?"

"I don't know. 9:30 maybe?"

"I think it was earlier."

"You feel it?"

"Maybe a little. You?" And just as he asked I felt it all at once. A rush of warmth straight to my chest. I felt it in between my pecs. I sighed.

"I think… it just hit me." I giggled. It was coming on quick.

"Oh… boy. Me too." Louie's features sagged. He leaned back against the wall. I did too. We waited.

Sometime later, Randy showed up. We were a mess by then, giggling and snorting. Randy was wearing a bizarre outfit. He had on a bright red onesie, and some sort of mask. A bright yellow lightning bolt was emblazoned on his chest. When he entered and saw us, we devolved into yet another fit of helpless laughter. He stepped around a few tables of drunk college guys, and sank into a chair across from me. The cushion had a hole in it. I had switched that chair with my chair earlier to avoid the hole. He shifted uncomfortably while he talked. His predicament made me laugh. I sipped the same cranberry juice I had been drinking since we got there. Isabel brought a drink over to the table next to us. I smiled at her. She looked at me like a mother looks at her son when he brings home a bad grade.

"Aw, shut the fuck up," Randy said before either of us spoke. Well, not before we laughed and pointed at the lightning bolt.

"Is it…Halloween?" I gasped, choking back tears.

"No, I was at a purim party." I grabbed Louie's watch and checked it. 10:32.

"How was it?" Louie laughed as he asked.

"It sucked." Each response only made us laugh harder. I put my head in my arms and folded them on the table. Randy looked at us.

"What's up with him?" he pointed me out to Louie, as if Louie was any better than I was. Louie looked at me and said, "He has terminal cancer." I whooped, spitting out my cranberry juice on Randy's costume. He jumped back, angry.

"It's okay," I said. "The colors match." Randy scowled at me.

"What are you, man?" Louie asked quietly out of the side of his mouth.

"The Flash," Randy answered. I laughed. Louie didn't. I turned and followed his eyes. In porn terms, a couple of barely legal busty coeds had strutted through the door. In fairy-tale terms, a few fair damsels had just taken the first step towards becoming distressed. Louie smoothed down his hair.

"You sure you're up for this Louie?" I asked. "You're pretty high."

"I am? I never thought of myself as pretty." I giggled. He was serious. Well, as serious as he could be in the situation. I licked my hand and ruffled his red cowlick.

"Stop it man. Cut it out. You coming with me?" I shook my head. Randy perked up.

"I will," he said. "Just let me get a drink." Isabel appeared as if summoned.

"What'll it be?" She asked.

"A waitress and a bartender?" I said. "What versatility." Isabel stared blankly at me. I smiled. She gave a small smile than looked to Randy.

"Let me get a whiskey sour." Isabel walked back to the bar. Louie tapped his foot. I hummed "A Dustland Fairytale." The girl at the table next to us looked over.

"Hello. I'm LeDarius McQuinton." She looked suspicious.

'I'm Jane," She said slowly. She looked towards the bathroom, as if she was waiting for a friend.

"Have you ever seen the rain, Jane?" She got up and moved to another table. Isabel brought Randy's drink over. The dark brown mixture was almost overflowing. He stood up and placed the drink on the table. He took out his wallet to pay.

"Okay, I'm ready." Louie stood up too. Their targets were being engaged by a different pride of lions. I kicked the table stand. Randy's drink spilled a little.

"Hey, man, chill." He grabbed his drink and slurped some off the sides of the glass.

"Whoopsies." I tickled Louie's belly. He tried not to laugh.

"Stop it."

"Just go," I said, "Before those ladies are snapped up by some other leading men." They walked carefully over, picking their way between tables, engaged in a discussion of the utmost importance. I surveyed the bar. It was a homogenous mix of white boys, white girls, and more white boys. The place itself was dark, with more tables than could be comfortably fit into such small place. The fake wooden chairs were spread all around, some tables had no chairs, and others had twice as many as they should. Those tables had invariably all female or all male occupants. The behavior of these groups depended on the sum of their Y chromosomes. The men all were on the prowl. At least one of them caught the eye of each girl that passed by. They spoke to each other only to formulate a game plan. They came here for one reason each night, to get fucked. The female tables, which were tables composed of females sitting at them, and not tables with female sexual reproductive organs, had a dichotomous purpose. Some of the girls looked around eagerly, gulping down bright blue drinks and pushing out their tits. They were here to get fucked. Others, particularly those who sat sipping on a glass of wine, looked around suspiciously, and often had a hand or two on their more eager friends. They had boyfriends, they were spoken for, they had found a mate and had no need to come to the local watering hole with all the other gazelles. They came here to make sure no one got fucked. The scent of desperation filled the bar. I loved it now. I'd hate it in the morning. Everywhere I looked I saw the funniest things I had ever seen in my short life.

A tall, strapping young lad made his way over to the table to my right, where a wench had sat and was intently staring at her phone. He engaged her in a conversation, which she reluctantly joined. He said something, and she twisted her hair around her finger. Then her phone flashed and she looked back down. Unperturbed, the Aryan sensation sat down next to her. *Aggresive*, I thought, *I'd avoid him on the Serengeti*. I eavesdropped by cupping a hand around my ear and leaning over. I don't think they saw me.

"Can I buy you a drink?"

"I'm actually waiting for my boyfriend." Ah, the two most dreaded words in the history of sleazy bars. "My boyfriend," which roughly translated to "There's already a penis in my life, and I'm not looking to add another one." Hercules stood up without another word and went back to his mates. They ribbed him a bit when he came back, I was sure.

I looked over to Louie and Randy. They were seated at their desired table, so they must have done alright for themselves. However, a closer look revealed three of the four women were texting, and the fourth was sipping water and glaring at them. The girl standing next to Louie stood up. She was unsteady. Her four-inch black heels clip-clopped as she made her way towards the bathroom. I figured I ought to help out my friends. I made my way to the bathroom. I also had to piss like a racehorse high on edibles. I tripped over the outstretched leg of some grey suit.

"Excuse me," the suit said.

"Well, when did we teach clothes to talk?" I eyeballed the empty discount suit wearily.

"What did you say, bro?" It stood up. It was almost human.

"My goodness! Is that you Phillip? My long-lost brother?" I laughed and turned away, humming the Rocky theme song. I raised my fists in triumph as I found Louie's target at the end of the line.

"Excuse me madam." She turned to me. She smiled. Women are horrible at flirting when they are this drunk. Good thing I wasn't here to flirt.

"What is your preferred moniker?"

"What?"

"What do the men shout out when they are with you?" I leaned against the grey wall, taking care not to cover the picture of Washington Square Park, 1886.

"I don't know…"

"Sweetheart, what's your name?" I sighed. Some people are dumb, others are smart.

"Karen." I took her hand. It was surprisingly mannish, with thick fingers and callouses in all the wrong places.

"Karen, my darling, I am Leonidas of Sparta. I was hoping you could inform me of the name of your friend over there drinking only water…" Her smile died. Her inferiority complex grew. "And the name of her boyfriend."

"How do you know she's got a boyfriend?" She was clearly confused. The experience of a man talking to her here with no desire to fuck her left her almost speechless. She began looking around for someone to take her home. We were almost to the front of the line.

"Look, toots, when a man's been leading safaris for this long, he learns to identify all species of the animal kingdom." I waved my hands as I talked. They looked like bluebirds. Or maybe sparrows. I was never good with bird names.

"Um, well she's Lauren. And her fiancé's name is William."

"Willy what?" She was reluctant. I gave her my most ingratiating smile and took her hand again. I stroked her ring finger to remind her she wasn't getting any younger. It was her turn for the bathroom.

"Willy what?"

"Jamison." She stumbled through the door to her left. A young Dominican gentleman with a chinstrap beard came out of the other one. He placed a bony hand on my chest and stood up as straight as he could. His Nirvana t-shirt stretched over his tiny chest.

"Hang on, man." His voice was lower than I expected. "There's a girl in there."

"Aw, yeah man. Look at you!" He smiled and walked past. I continued. "Who fucked a drunk slut in a grimy bathroom? You did! Go Pablo!" I walked after him. He saw me follow and sped up. I wasn't trailing him. I detoured over to Louie and Randy and Lauren's table. I sat down next to the only person whose name I didn't know. I became frantic.

"Are you Lauren?" I asked her.

"No," she said. She looked at the real Lauren. They were apprehensive. "William Jamison's girl?" I asked. I looked at the goalie. With any luck, I'd be able to pull her and give my friends some time on an empty net.

"That's me," she said. "Who are you?"

I took a deep breath. "I'm Roger. Will's probably mentioned me. No? He hasn't? Well, it doesn't matter now. We were out drinking tonight and he was mugged. He's in bad shape. He asked for you, but none of us had your number."

"Wait, but he's been texting me." She looked down at her phone.

"I think that might be the guy who mugged him. Look, we can figure it out. The point is, he's in Washington Square Park right now asking for you. He told me you were here, showed me a picture he carries, and asked me to get you."

"Omigod. I'll be right there." She grabbed her purse and kissed her girlfriend on the cheek. I followed her as she went out the door, then grabbed her arm, maybe a little roughly.

"Are you nuts?" She wasn't even drunk.

"What?"

"You're about to follow a random stranger to an empty park in the middle of the night?" She tensed up. I was between her and the door.

"William's fine. I don't even know him. I just wanted to help my friends."

"You asshole! You fucking asshole!" Her tiny fists started hitting me. I snickered.

"C'mon! You were like Marty Brodeur over there! I needed to set a screen." She looked at me, incredulous.

"Asshole," she muttered again. She stormed back inside. I pulled out a cigarette. I needed to chase the high. A scary-looking Mexican man walked past. He asked for a cigarette. I have one rule in this city-- if someone asks for a cigarette, I give them one. I lit his and then mine. He took off. I wasn't in the mood to shoot the shit. Was I really better than Louie and Randy? I didn't creep on girls sitting at tables to get them to sleep with me, but I did just lie to a woman that her fiancé was in danger to try and get her friends to sleep with my friends. If that's not stage one behavior, I don't know what is. I threw down the half-smoked cigarette and stomped it out. I went back inside. It hadn't even worked. Randy and Louie were waiting for me at our original table. I sat back down. None of us said a word. I checked my phone. Nothing from Amanda. I typed out a message to her, but didn't send it. My bladder reminded me that, like Amanda, its needs had not been met.

An hour or three later, I was sobering up.

"I'm not even high anymore." I turned to Randy and Louie. They were exhausted from a night of rejection. "I need a drink."

"I know where we can get one." Randy started smiling. I hailed a cab.

"I'm not walking anywhere." I said. I got in. Louie joined me. Randy pointed to the sign on top of the cab.

"Take us there please." The cabbie nodded. Randy got in next to Louie. I placed my forehead against the cool glass and reached into my pocket. I squeezed the stress ball while we drove. The lights from buildings blurred together, and before I knew it we were there. At the strip club. I didn't even know the name. We shuffled out, Randy and Louie excited, me thirsty. We showed our ID's to the large black man working the door. "Head on in, fellas." He pulled the red rope back and waved us in. We traipsed past the underage high schoolers who had thought for sure that their fakes would let them see boobies, even though they had more red marks on their faces than Tina Turner after a fight with Ike. They stared at us with envy as we entered the world of shaking and ogling.

The smell of cheap champagne washed over us. I looked around for a bottle, eager to drink the night away. A black-haired girl wearing a v-shaped onesie with enormous fake tits came over.

"I'm Misty." She spoke through her nose. "Can I get you boys anything?"

I reached into my pocket for my wallet. It felt thinner than normal, and I realized that I hadn't brought any cash, to prevent high me from spending too much. *Sober Zach is such an asshole*, I thought, even though I was almost him at that point.

"Buy me a drink," I told Randy, who shook his head. His eyes were on a thin redhead up on the nearest pole. She bent over and flipped her hair up, catching Randy's eye.

"No way man, I need to save this money for important things." The song ended. The redhead hopped off the stage, landing gracefully on her fuck-me heels. Randy eagerly waved her over. Two other strippers came as well, evening up the sides.

"Hello, I'm Naomi, would you like a private dance?" She placed her hands on Randy's shoulders. He salivated. Her eyes didn't smile nearly as wide as her mouth. Randy wasn't looking at her eyes, or her mouth for that matter. He nodded, and placed a twenty in between her breasts. She straddled him. One of the other girls, the blond, approached me.

"Hello, I'm Olive, would you like a private dance?" She placed her hands on my shoulders. The similarity in approach between her and Randy's redhead was creepy. I shook my head.

"No money," was all I said. She frowned and moved towards Louie, but the brunette was already there.

"Hey baby, I like your hair. How 'bout a dance? I'm Paris." Louie looked her over. He wanted to, that was clear. But he also didn't have any money.

"Could we work out some kind of… payment plan?" I cracked up. Had he really just said that? Paris left. Louie ran his hands through his ginger hair and looked over at Randy, who was thoroughly enjoying Naomi's company. He looked at me. I pointed at another table. We took a seat in front of a pole. A large black girl came out. "Introducing Quinn!" A Russian man with a thick accent said into a microphone. One guy clapped. A bunch got up and moved to another table.

"I'm too not high for this." I turned away from the large girl who had removed her robe and begun to gyrate. "Why the fuck they got Precious up there?"

"Wait." Louie had his hands in his pockets. "I just realized I have something that might help."

"What is it? I'll do anything right now." I leaned forward and rested my chin on my hands. Louie placed a small baggie of white powder on the table.

"What the fuck is that?" I got up. My voice was too loud.

"It's just coke," Louie said. I wanted to hit him.

"Just coke, you fucking asshole? Just coke?" I grabbed his collar and pulled him towards me.

Louie understood his mistake and took back the coke. It wasn't worth it, I decided. I pushed him back down. I felt tears, so I got up and left without another word. I walked briskly home. It started to drizzle. I walked faster. It started to rain. I began jogging, then running. A block from my apartment, I heard a crash of thunder and it began pouring buckets of rain. I stopped moving and looked up. I was soaked. I had never been more sober.

"I'm 24 years old. I hate my job, I hate my friends, and I spend every night getting too fucked up to think about it." I spoke to no one. I walked inside. "And the only woman I've ever loved dumped me because I said she snores too much," I whispered to myself as I unlocked my apartment and went it. I looked at my "home." It was a collection of Ikea furniture and bare walls. There was nothing personal to it. I had a TV, a computer, and a bong. They were all I had to show for six years living away from home. I hadn't truly had a home since I came home for winter break my freshman year and my parents had moved to the other side of town. We were moving up in the world, but I wasn't really coming along. I sighed, then the tears I had felt came out. I cried for the first time in fifteen years. I stopped holding back. Big, racking, sobs came out of me. I grabbed an empty bottle of vodka off the cheap Ikea table and threw it at the wall. It shattered into a million tiny pieces. I searched desperately through piles of dirty clothes, hoping for a dub, a pill, anything to take the edge off, to close Pandora's box. I couldn't deal with it. I couldn't find anything. I retreated to my favorite chair in the corner. I sat in it and looked at the mess I had made, had been making, had stuck myself in. The tears finally stopped. I was out. I wiped my eyes with the back of my hands and closed my eyes. Images of Amanda and Brian assaulted my brain. I pulled my hair and screamed. I cursed. I flashed back to that night…

A text. It's Brian. We made plans to meet up, like we always did. He said he had something good for tonight. He'd been weird lately. Distant. Never seemed to be where we were. He was always off in some special place. I texted Amanda, but she was swamped with briefs to read. I figured I better put on some pants. I threw the joint I was smoking out the window. I was buzzed, but not high. I walked to the bathroom and looked in the mirror. Mirror Zach, with two-days-too-many growth, stared back from inside the glass. I put my hand up against his. He smiled. I laughed. I reached for my razor and shaved just the mustache. He looked better now, I decided. I flexed my abs and was satisfied with how he looked shirtless. I brushed my teeth for the first time of the day. I spit out the bright blue paste and washed out my mouth. Another text. Amanda. She said she might join us later.

I looked for the best smelling pair of jeans on the mountain of clothes in my tiny bedroom. I could touch every wall in the room from my bed. I found a pair with no food on them. I sniffed. Smelled like denim, just like it should, with just a hint of mustard. I pulled them on, taking care with the zipper to not catch anything extra. I headed for the door, but noticed in the reflection of the stainless steel toaster that my grandmother had given me as a You Live Alone Now gift that I had a stain on my shirt. Fuck. I went back to the mountain and found a faded Hendrix shirt. I loved the freedom of having a girlfriend. I barely had to care what I wore; I knew I was getting laid anyways.

I headed out the door. "So what we smoke weeeed," I sang to myself as I walked down the four flights of stairs and out the front door. My next-door neighbor Mrs. Johnson was coming in, carrying Jefferson, her orange tabby cat, with her. The cat hissed at me. Mrs. Johnson sang the next lyric: "So what we do druuuugs." I smiled at her. She was in her late thirties, but unlike most people her age she didn't resent my generation for being young enough to still have fun. We sang the rest in unison as we walked away from each other. "We're just havin' fuuun." I jumped over a trash bag that had been moved to the middle of the sidewalk.

Waka Flaka Flame was blasting when Brian opened the door. He wore slacks and a navy button-down with the top three buttons undone, revealing some sparse chest hair and a few moles. He stroked his new beard as I came in.

"When you gonna shave that thing?" I greeted him with a bro hug. Clasp hands and pull in, then pat on the back once.

"When it stops drivin' girls wild." He took a big bite out of a red delicious he was holding. "So probably never." He spoke with his mouth full and little flecks of apple came out. We both tried to keep a straight face before cracking up. Brian was a ladies' man in the least frat-boy way possible. Killed 'em with kindness, or something like that. "You want something to eat?" he asked after he had finished chewing.

"You got any of those chewy bars?" I walked past him to the kitchen to find out for myself. A frying pan was on the stove, its handle facing out. I stepped past it carefully and opened the cabinet above the stove.

"Trying to eat healthy?" Brian followed me. He grabbed a silver tray off the counter that separated the kitchen from the living room. He held it up to me.

"Of course. Gotta stay fit for Amanda." I looked down at the perfectly organized lines. I pushed in my left nostril with my pointer finger and leaned down. Pffffft. I wiped my nose and opened the chewy bar I found.

"She coming tonight?" Brian snorted a line of coke off the tray. He picked up his apple and took a few big bites. His cheeks puffed out like a squirrel. His nose was red. He hadn't just started.

"Not till later. We got some time." I gestured for the tray. He handed it over. I snorted another line.

"Hey man, you mind throwing for this? Shit's mad expensive and I haven't worked in a few weeks." Brian took the tray back.

"Course man." I threw a twenty on the counter. Brian snatched it quickly. He didn't give me any change. "What happened to that commercial you auditioned for?"

"Shit was weird. I went in, right, and nailed the fucking thing. It was for the part of Son, okay?" Brian was animated as he talked, waving his hands and the tray around, a little coke spilled off the edge onto the table.

"Okay, easy man, don't spill that shit." I put my pointer finger on the coke and lifted it. It stuck.

"And I do everything great, I mean the dude was almost crying after a few takes. I really got into it." I sucked the coke off my finger.

"So what happened?" I felt my pulse begin to race. Brian stood up and walked over to the window. He looked out.

"The guy says, 'that was great. Unfortunately, you're a little old for the part.'" Brian turned back to me. "Now, I know I'm out of college, but have you seen the kids they have playing high schoolers? Minka Kelly played a high school sophomore while dating Derek fucking Jeter."

"How old was the character?" I took a bite of the chewy bar. It tasted like walnuts. I looked at the packaging. Fuck. I took the wrong one.

"That's what I asked. They tell me he's supposed to be eight to ten years old." I burst out laughing. Brian scowled, then grinned. "Now, they had a headshot of me, they had my resume. They knew how old I was."

"And when you got there." I was laughing so hard. I doubled over. "They still had you do the lines even though you were--"

"24 fucking years old." Brian started laughing too. I did another line. He walked over and did another line. He started laughing again and blew some of it out his nose. He had powder all over his face. I cracked up all over again. He laughed, and licked around his lips to salvage as much of it as he could. I grabbed a towel that was next to the sink and threw it at his face. He let it hit, then kept it there with one hand. He was wearing a large fake diamond on his pinky.

"So what did you have that's so good tonight?" I asked, finally calming down. My cheeks hurt from laughing so hard. The fluttering feeling in my chest intensified.

"Besides this?" Brian did another line. I did too.

"Yeah, besides this." I could feel my heart beating, pumping the oxygenated blood around my body.

"There's this thing out in a warehouse in Brooklyn." There were two lines left. Brian looked at me.

"All you," I said. I had had enough. I jumped and touched the ceiling.

'We're going to a rave? Really? Is it freshman year again?" I looked around as if we had been sent back in time and I was trying to figure out what had happened.

"I know the guy throwing it." Brian did a line. Pffft. His nose was really red.

"Great, what's that mean?" I put my hands up like a boxer. Brian laughed and held up his hands to me open. I punched his right with my right and his left with my left, then ducked. He took each hit and then swung over my head. "I'm too quick."

"We get in for free, and we get free drinks." I did the Ali shuffle. Brian went to the fridge and took out a beer. He tossed it to me. I snagged it and popped the top off against the counter.

"Drink that quick, I want to go. Just let me use the bathroom first." I drank deeply. God, I loved beer. Brian disappeared into the bathroom and slammed the door. I jumped at the noise. I spilled a little beer on my shirt. I called Amanda.

"What's up babe?" She sounded tired and distracted.

"You coming tonight?"

"I don't think I'll be able to."

"Damn, you sound so sexy when you turn me down."

"Where you guys going?"

"We're going to a rave because Brian knows the guy who is throwing the rave and we are going to have a lot of fun because we get to go for free and drink for--"

"Woah, slow down. Are you okay, Zach?" I chugged the rest of the beer.

"I'm fine. We had a little, y'no."

"Why, Zach? Don't you think you shouldn't encourage him?"

"He's a grown man, okay? If he wants to he can. And when I want to, which isn't often, I can too, okay?"

"Alright, alright, calm down. I just don't like it."

"I hope you can make it, text me when you finish."

"Okay, have fun."

I hung up. I realized I didn't say goodbye. I hoped she didn't mind. I thought she probably didn't want to talk to me anyway, she had a lot of work. *She works so slowly*, I thought, *Not like me*. She was a lot more thorough though. She had better grades than me in high school. I saw her old transcripts once. I did better on the SAT's though. I heard a crash come from the bathroom. I ran over to the door and banged on it.

'What's goin' on in there?" I spoke in a funny accent. Brian opened the door. His hand was bleeding, his eyes were blood-shot.

"I punched the mirror," he said. I looked at him. He looked at me. I laughed, and went over to get the towel, which was still resting on the counter where he had left it. I tossed it to him. He wiped off the blood and went back into the bathroom to get a band-aid. He came out a few seconds later and brushed his hair behind his ears. He looked like Tim Riggins, or whatever the guy who played him was named. "Let's go," he said.

We saw the warehouse and both basically ran there. I had so much energy. "That's it, right?" I asked.

"Yep yep yep." He got there before me. We slowed and approached the bouncer. There was a line of about fifteen people waiting to pay.

"Excuse me," Brian jumped in front of two college girls wearing neon tank tops and clearly rolling on Molly. They let him in front of them and looked at me with a dazed expression. I smiled and giggled. Brian addressed the bouncer, a surprisingly thin white guy with a scraggly beard and large Jew-fro. "We are friends of Dimitri's," he said. "My name is Brian Lewis." The bouncer checked his list. He handed us 21+ wristbands and nodded. We skipped past him in to the warehouse. MGMT was playing. The MDMA girls watched us go, and one of them smiled at me. *She must not have seen Brian*, I thought.

The place was absolutely packed. Everyone there was on Molly or speed or cocaine. The music was so loud it sounded like it was inside my skull. I counted three couples violently making out within ten feet of the entrance. The only dancing being done was grinding, and everyone was dancing. I screamed with delight and followed Brian, who shoved his way past one particularly intimate couple. The guy took his hand out of the girl's pants and turned after us. She had blond hair in her eyes and was mindlessly pumping her fist and leaning on him. He had sharp eyebrows and angry cheekbones, and looked ready to fight. *Uh oh*, I thought. Just as I prepared to Ali shuffle his ass to death, the girl took his hand and placed it back down her very short skirt. He consented, and a crisis was averted. I caught up to Brian. He was talking to the bouncer of the VIP section, which was just a dance floor elevated two stairs above the regular person dance floor with its own bar. Two Asian girls danced on tables, wearing matching black trash bags and nothing else.

"Brian Lewis!" Brian shouted at the bouncer, a more appropriately sized, for such a position, white man with a bald spot and bad teeth. He checked the list and nodded, but when Brian attempted to pass, put a hand on his chest.

"VIP's ABC." He gestured at the girls. Anything But Clothes. Oh well.

"It's fine!" I pulled Brian away from the VIP area. We started dancing. After about two seconds, two tall brunettes approached. Brian grabbed one. The other eyed me. I smiled, and danced. She tried to grind with me. I resisted. Brian spotted two floaters at a nearby table (the only table in sight in the whole place) and drained one. He gave me the other. I drank it. *What the hell*, I figured, *Dancing never hurt anyone.* I grabbed the girl and she squealed with delight.

We danced the night away. Occasionally Brian would head off to the bathroom. He would shoot me a glance each time but I'd shake my head. I didn't use much, so I didn't need nearly as much to feel amazing as Brian did. I explained to each girl I danced with that my girlfriend was meeting me there, and suggested they speak with my more-handsome friend when he returned from the bathroom. At first, most took me up on the offer, and Brian danced and hooked up with several girls. I lived vicariously, and was enjoying myself. As the night went on, Brian looked more and more deranged. His nostrils were more and more red, his hair was a mess, and he had undone his shirt all the way down to the last button. While he wasn't the worst there, the girls I turned down no longer agreed with my assessment of our attractiveness.

Around 2:00 or so, I suggested to Brian that we call it a night. He weakly said sure, and we left. He put his arm around me as we traversed the wooden dance floor for the last time. The crowd had thinned, but the place was still packed. Pairs of men and women were leaving in a steady stream out the door, and pairs of men and pairs of women were also exiting. As this was Brooklyn, the pairs of men were the handsiest with each other.

"I love you, man." He was slurring his words pretty badly. I started to worry a little.

"I love you too, bud. Are you okay?" His eyes were half-open. I shook him.

"Yeah, I'm fine, let's just go home." We took the elevator down into the subway. I swiped for both of us. A group of fellow ravers looked at us. I smiled. One of the girls was leaning against the wall. She had dim blue eyes and looked sick. Her friend was talking to her in a quiet voice. We exchanged empathetic looks.

The train came. Brian and I walked as one into the last car. We sat down. Sitting seemed to do him some good. He had perked up by the time we got to 8th St. Station. He wanted to get some halal food. I convinced him to wait. Or I thought I did. As we exited, he ran ahead to the nearest cart and ordered lamb and rice.

"You like workin' here?" He attempted to engage the Middle-Eastern man making his food. The guy wanted none of it, but felt obligated to respond.

" 's OK." The meat sizzled as it cooked.

"How long you in here for?" Brian stood obnoxiously close to the cart, his nose peering over the window at the food.

"It's not prison, Brian." I tried to get him to take a step back.

"I mean, how long are your shifts?" Brian took out his wallet.

"8 hours or so, depending on the night." The man scooped yellow rice into a Styrofoam container. He had a bushy mustache and a dark mark on his right temple. He looked like he hadn't slept in weeks. "You want sauce?"

All of a sudden, Brian looked worse. "White sauce." I spoke for Brian. I stepped forward and he put his arm around me again. I took Brian's wallet and opened it. It was empty. Sighing, I took out my wallet and paid the man. He eyed Brian.

"He okay?"

"He's fine. Just give me that." That was good enough for him. He had no desire to get involved. No one in this city ever did. He handed over the food. We stumbled the few blocks back to Brian's apartment.

Brian insisted on taking the stairs when we got back. I didn't mind, I felt recharged. I had stolen a few bites of lamb on the way. Well, not really stolen, considering I paid for it. We ran up the six flights to his apartment. Brian was way ahead of me.

When I got to the top, Brian was heading down. I stopped him with a hand. "Where are you going?"

Panting, he responded, "I dropped my keys, I think. A few flights down, I'll be back in a bit." I sat on the top stair and took at the halal. I had eaten half of it by the time he came back. Sweat poured down his face. "Got 'em." He opened the door and let me in first.

I was always surprised at how clean Brian kept things, especially in comparison to me. But at times like this I appreciated it. I sat down on the couch. Brian turned on the TV. We watched some shitty movie on Comedy Central in silence. Brian seemed to be coming down. He gave one word answers to any questions I asked. He took the halal and finished it in about thirty seconds.

I got up and went to the bathroom. It was a complete mess. The mirror was completely broken. Blood was all over the sink and tiled floor. A sign with illustrations depicting the proper use of a toilet seat that normally hung above the toilet was in the shower. The shower curtain had been pulled off the rings, presumably as Brian tried to stop himself from falling over. *What was he doing in here?* I peed and washed my hands. I watched myself in the broken mirror. Bits and pieces of my face and hands were visible in the remaining shards of glass. I looked okay, I decided. Better than Brian, anyway.

When I came back, Brian was asleep. He was slumped in a weird position. I felt his head to make sure he was okay. He wasn't breathing. I freaked out. I started running around the room looking for a phone, but he didn't have a phone and I didn't know what to do and I was going to yell out the window for an ambulance when I remembered I had a cell phone. I took it out and dialed 922, cursed, and dialed 911.

"911, what is your emergency?" The deep voice surprised me. In the movies, it's always a woman answering. I explained that my friend had OD'd and I needed an ambulance. I became strangely calm. I answered all their questions, but I wasn't there. I watched from above as I set him as they described, and put the pillow where I was told. I noticed the half-line of coke that he had while I was in the bathroom and couldn't finish. I saw the next few hours playing out: the desperate journey to the hospital, the waiting and waiting, Amanda meeting me at the hospital, the stern looking doctor in blue scrubs coming out and explaining to us while scratching his beard and shaking his head that he hadn't made it.

And that's what happened. I re-watched it like a movie as I sat alone in my apartment. I did the only thing that made sense at the time. I called my mother. She didn't answer. I thought of how Brian died alone. I called my mother again. She picked up.

"You better have a damn good reason for waking us up at this hour."

"I'll meet her."

"What?" She was confused. Her voice was groggy and irritated.

"I'll meet that girl. The one you told me about."

"Zoey?" I stood up and began pacing.

"Yeah, I think. The one you said would be perfect for me. I'll meet her."

"Great, outstanding. I'm so glad you called me to tell me that."

"So what's her number?"

"You want me to get out of bed and track down the number of a girl I offered to get for you a few days ago and you blew me off?"

"Please, Mom?"

"I'll text you in the morning. Calling her now would ruin any chance you have. I love you."

"I love you too, Mom."

She hung up without commenting on my deviation from our normal goodbye. I wiped my eyes. I suddenly realized I was absolutely exhausted. I fell asleep in my chair completely dressed.

Chapter 5

Amanda pulls me on top of her. We're naked and going at it like rabbits. She tells me how glad she is to have me back. I cover her mouth with my hand. She pushes it off and keeps talking. She says how even though I'm not great in bed she loves me anyways. I cover my ears with my hands. My mother walks into the room. I try to pull away, but Amanda wraps her legs around my back and pulls me closer. I look at my mother. Amanda starts moaning and shrieking. My mother tells me she's faking. Edward, her new husband, walks in wearing a Speedo. I'm repulsed by his gray and black chest hair. His pecs wrinkle as he puts his arm around my mother. Amanda screams louder. "Brian!" She screams the name of my dead best friend and looks me in the eyes. My father walks in. His skin has started to rot. I can see his thigh bones as he walks. They are pearly white. His face is decomposing. He looks at me with dead eyes. He tells me I'm doing it wrong. Edward walks over and smacks my dad. He crumbles, literally crumbles. A pile of bones and dust are left in his place. Amanda finishes. She releases me. I try to run out, but there are no doors. They all laugh at me.

* * *

I woke up in a cold sweat. The bright orange lights beneath the TV read 12:32. Shit. I was meeting Amanda at 1. I showered quickly, with no time to enjoy the feel of the hot water rushing over me. I toweled off and looked in the mirror. My hair was sticking up. It wouldn't stay down no matter how many different ways I smoothed it over. I resolved to get a haircut after lunch, provided I wasn't having make-up sex all day. I also noticed a small zit was appearing in between my eyebrows. I pushed it. It got redder. *Goddammit.* I ran out of the bathroom to my closet. I put on a pair of khaki pants and a white button-down. I put on my peacoat even though it wasn't that cold because I didn't want to show up wearing a hoodie. I guess I suspected part of the reason she dumped me was because I looked like a slob so often. Though it probably had more to do with me being an asshole. I remembered that I dumped her. That helped. I felt better.

I saw Mrs. Johnson as I left. She was walking Jefferson as if he were a dog. She had a bright red leash tied around his neck and he was sitting there, just looking at her. He seemed to find the idea of walking for the sake of walking ridiculous. I agreed.

"Zach, where are you rushing off to?" She examined her nails. The polish was chipped and old.

"I don't have time to explain, I'm late." I rushed past her.

"Wait." She was nonplussed. "You buttoned your shirt wrong." I looked down, she was right.

"Thanks," I said to her. "You are a fucking moron who will die alone," I said to me. I ran off, unfastening and refastening as I did so. The restaurant was just far enough that it was faster to walk than take the subway, but was still a long walk. I cut through Washington Square Park. "You want some bud man?" A tall black guy said in my general direction. I shook my head and pushed past him. The park was remarkably crowded for March, but it was a Sunday. A few street performers were loudly describing the great trick they were about to perform. A crowd had gathered around the fountain to watch. But first, they were going to come around for donations.

I walked around all of these people and the arch caught my eye. A bunch of caution tape was up around a part of its base. I figured that had something to do with the piece that had fallen off a few days ago. No one had been hurt. I imagined being killed by a piece falling off the arch. All the energy, all the work of so many people that had gone into making me who I was would have been for naught. I wouldn't have died for some noble cause. No one would remember me for anything other than my bizarre cause of death, and even that wouldn't last. Killed by a statue, they would say. Eventually it would just become another fun fact about one of the many tourist attractions in this tourist trap of a city. As I passed the old men challenging anyone and everyone to a game of chess, I wondered who would miss me. My mother, sure, but she didn't count. Amanda, maybe. Kevin, probably. The rest of my friends at least for awhile. But then I'd just be like Brian. We'd probably be clumped together. Both our deaths, and by association our lives, would become one event, that they would reflect on when the right combination of alcohol and weed made them nostalgic.

I checked my phone for the time. I had ten minutes to get to the diner. I needed to stop depressing myself. I had to appear happy, okay without Amanda. I bought a cup of coffee. I drank as quickly as its temperature would allow as I made my way up West 4th.

Amanda was already seated when I came in. I walked past the hostess and made my way to her table. She stood up when she saw me. She looked great. She was wearing a conservative blouse and jeans, but even so it was obvious how pretty she was. She half-smiled when she saw me. The moment of truth arrived-- how would we greet each other? Certainly not a kiss, but a handshake would be awkward and weird. She hugged me, gently wrapping her arms around my neck. She held her sleeves with her hands while she did. I put one arm around her waist and leaned in, trying to be even more casual than she was.

"Thanks for coming." She sat down and picked up the menu.

"No problem. I am so sorry I'm late." I sat down opposite her. A waitress came over. Her hair was pulled tightly back into a neat bun. She looked bored.

"You guys want to start off with something to drink?"

Amanda pointed to the menu. "I'll have orange juice." She looked at me. I realized my eyes had drifted downwards on the waitress. I did my best to cover by reading her name-tag.

"Yes... Rebecca, I'll have a ... tea, if you have it." I looked from her to the menu to her to Amanda.

"How do you want that?" Neither of them noticed how hyper I was.

"Sorry?" She put her hand that was holding her notepad on her hip and looked down at me.

"Sugar, lemon…"

"Oh, right. Nothing, please." She wrote something down, probably a note to stay away from our table as much as possible, and walked off. I looked around. Sports paraphernalia, most of it Jets-related, covered the walls. I shuddered, I hated the Jets. Amanda had sat facing the door, presumably so she could clock exactly how late I was. I checked my phone. I wasn't even late. I was unnerved, I liked to sit facing the door. There weren't too many other diners in the restaurant. Still, there were enough restauranteurs in the diner that it would be awkward if we fought.

"So how are you?" She apparently was sick of the silence. I refocused on her, making sure to meet her eyes. The choice of blouse helped. Still, I knew exactly what she looked like naked, so I could see her naked whenever I wanted to if I felt like it. It was a sort of intoxicating power, knowing someone so intimately that whatever shield or facade they put on you could cut right through.

"I'm doing well. Yourself?" I opened the menu as nonchalantly as possible. The last thing I wanted was for her to think I was chalant. That would end any chance we had of getting back together.

"Riiight. I'm okay." She kept looking at me looking at the menu. She tapped her foot.

"Good. Have you been here before? I don't know what to get." Wrong question. She leaned forward and opened her mouth, then closed it. She wanted to yell. But she was raised a good girl, and she knew always to act like a lady in public. So she settled herself. When she spoke, it was in the loudest, angriest whisper I had ever heard.

"You don't get to come in here and make…. Fucking small talk, okay? You owe me an apology. I didn't want that night to be the last time we ever spent together."

I looked at her, my face neutral. She leaned back.

"I'm sorry," I said. I meant it too. "You're right. We were good friends long before we ever started dating, it would be a shame if we had to stop seeing each other just because you won't marry me."

"You really think we broke up because of that proposal?" She leaned back in. Her condescension irritated me. I smiled at her.

"No, I broke up with you because of your snoring." Body blow. She almost recoiled.

"I'll ignore that. We both know I broke up with you. You want to know why? Because you fucking hate yourself. You haven't forgiven yourself for Brian's death, you think it was your fault. You're terrified you'll end up alone, when two months ago you would have laughed at the idea of marrying me, or anyone. But now you're terrified at the idea of having only yourself to talk to, because you hate everything you think. So you drug yourself to avoid thinking. We broke up because I can't do that anymore. I can't ever love you when you hate yourself so much. And no one can." She leaned back. She was out of breath.

I leaned in. "You know what? You--" Rebecca was back. I stopped talking and smiled pleasantly up at her and her magnificent tits.

"Are you ready to order?" She placed our drinks on the table and took her notepad out.

"I'll have a burger and fries, and she'll have a salad." Rebecca's eyebrows raised at my ordering for Amanda, and Amanda seethed but said nothing. She scrawled our orders down and walked away. I grinned malevolently at Amanda. "I've always wanted to do that. And now I can. We're such cliches, I thought it was fitting. Because you're right, I do blame myself for Brian's death. And you can tell yourself all that crap about being unable to love me because of me and all that, but we both know that's utter bullshit. Let me tell you why you can't love me." The people at the table next to us looked over. I leaned back and gripped the metal chair to calm down. Amanda waited.

"You can't love me because you blame me, Amanda. You think I should have cut him off, should have realized what happened and gotten him to a hospital sooner. You will never love me because of that. And I can't say I blame you. I wish every day that he was still here, that I had done something differently." I stood up and dropped my napkin on the table. I was done. I had verbalized a feeling that had bothered me since Wednesday. I had figured out what happened to us. A weight lifted off of me. Not the big one, but one of the smaller ones. Amanda was crying. I didn't care anymore. I threw two twenties on the table. "Enjoy your meal. I hope someday we can be friends. I really mean that. You were a wonderful part of my life for a long time." I turned away. So much for not making a scene. Every pair of eyes in the place followed me except Lou's, the blind chef.

"Zach…" I turned. Amanda looked at me, tears in her bright blues eyes. I waited. She opened her mouth. She brushed her hair out of her eyes and tucked it behind her ear. She closed her mouth. I left.

My phone vibrated as I was unlocking my door. I stepped inside and tossed my keys on the table. I unbuttoned my peacoat with one hand and pulled out my phone with the other. It was a message from my mom. "Zoey's number," it read, followed by a string of digits. I paused. Was Amanda right? Maybe I wasn't ready for this. If this girl was everything my mother said, maybe I wasn't being fair to introduce myself at such a bad time in my life and drag her down with me. Then again, I've always been selfish. If calling her had a chance of making me happy, why should I pass it up? I'd never even met her. I dialed the first digit when my phone vibrated. It was Kevin. He wanted me to meet up with him for dinner. "Sure." I texted back. I realized I hadn't checked my email in a few days. I had nothing but spam. A nice woman named Sylvia had written to tell me how I could enlarge my penis and satisfy her for hours. I was flattered, but not particularly interested.

A few hours later I remembered I hadn't called Zoey yet. I figured I'd do it after dinner. Kevin had texted me nothing but an address, so I googled it to find out where and what it was. Some Italian place up in Midtown. Seemed kind of far for us to meet for dinner. Expensive too. He must have some sort of ulterior motive, I figured. As long as he didn't try to have a heart-to-heart, I'd be fine. And if he wanted to buy me an expensive dinner, who was I to stop him?

I got there at 7:15. Kevin had said 7, but he was always late. Except this time. The maitre'd laughed when I told her I was meeting the most uptight guy wearing the most conservative suit in the place.

"I know exactly who you're talking about. This way." I watched her ass as I walked behind her. It swayed left and right. She was a little older, maybe early forties, late thirties, but I didn't mind.

"Here we are. Let me know if you need anything. I'm Talia." I watched her walk away. Kevin was wearing a black suit with a white tie. With his pale skin and black crew-cut, the only splotch of color anywhere on him were his lips, which were pursed. He gestured impatiently for me to sit down.

"You're finally here." He grabbed my arm and made me sit next to him. For the first time I noticed there were four chairs at the table, and two of them were already pulled out.

"What is this?" I asked.

"The ladies are in the bathroom," he continued, talking over me. Then he seemed to hear my question.

"You remember that girl I told you about?"

"The one you banged last weekend?" He shushed me. I looked around and admired all the nice clothes the other people there had on. I was woefully underdressed.

"I've had dinner with her a few times. I actually kind of like her so please don't mess this up." He calmed down. I didn't.

"Then why am I here? Who's the other girl?" I realized what this was. "Oh. Kevin. Tell me this isn't a double date. Please." I put my head in my arms on the table and looked up at him.

"What do you want me to say?" He scratched the top of his head. I wished his hair was longer so I could pull it.

"I want you to tell me that this isn't a blind date, and I want that to be the truth."

"Excuse me gentlemen." It was the waitress. She was an old, old woman. I was surprised she could walk. Her breasts had long ago given up on fighting their losing battle with gravity. She seemed like a brisk wind could pick her up and carry her off to heaven. But her voice was strong. It startled me. I sat up and folded my hands in my lap. "Now that the last member of your party is here, I was wondering if you might like a drink?" She looked at me.

"Yes, um, I'd like a glass of chardonnay I guess." She didn't write anything down.

"Very well. Sir, would you like another?" She indicated Kevin's beer with a nod.

"Yes, please, ma'am." Kevin also seemed unnerved.

"I'll have those for you in a few, and perhaps then every member of your party will actually be at the table?"

"Thank you, uh, what did you say your name was?" Kevin seemed oddly interested.

"Ursula, dear." Her tone made it clear that she didn't feel he was particularly dear to her or anyone. I laughed.

"Is that your real name?" She frowned at me. Her face could not wrinkle any deeper, so she had to lower her eyebrows to make it clear she was upset.

"No, it's the stage name I use to keep away my fans." Her tone was so dry and bored that I had trouble detecting she was kidding for a few seconds. After neither of us responded, she turned and shuffled away. I turned back to Kevin.

"Is this really a blind date? Why would you do that to me?"

"Uh, well…" He wasn't looking at me. I followed his eyes to the two beautiful ladies exiting the restroom. They were laughing as they strode through the place. Every single head that was attached to a body that was attached to a penis turned as they did so. A few that weren't turned too.

"Which one are you dating?" Not that it mattered, I'd have the blond or the redhead.

"The redhead," he whispered. "Her name's Violet." Damn. I wanted the oxymoronic one.

"What's mine named?"

"Wanda." I turned back, content now that I had a name to put to the face. And damn was it a nice face. Her red lips curled as she laughed, and her round amber eyes twinkled. The rest wasn't too bad either. Her legs went on for miles. She wore a red frilly dress that would have looked foolish on most other girls, including Amanda. I stood up as they got to our table. Kevin followed suit.

"Violet, this is Zach." we shook hands. Her handshake was surprisingly firm. "Zach, this is Wanda." She placed her hand in mine daintily. I kissed it. She giggled.

"Please, I prefer Cosmo." Kevin snickered. They just stared at me. Not a great start. Ursula came back with my wine and Kevin's beer. She took our orders. I felt the strange need to have her approve of my order. I went with a steak. The way she repeated it made me feel I had erred.

"She is so creepy," Wanda said as she walked away.

"Yeah," I said. "It's so weird to think she was our age once, going out on dates and partying and stuff. I wonder if you'll be like that when you're older."

Wanda's face warped. Kevin grimaced. "You think I'll look like that? Well, you must not think much of me now."

"No! I didn't mean it that way at all. I meant... you're so beautiful now, and I just thought... wouldn't it be weird if in fifty years..." my voice trailed off. It was over. I had lost. That's the thing with first impressions-- they're all that matter, and they're based on such tiny intervals of time that a momentary lapse in judgement can cost you an entire relationship. The rest of the dinner would be a waste of time. The weird thing is, we're expected to act so perfectly normal when we meet someone. But no one is looking for "normal." Everyone is looking for someone unique, someone who will tell us things that only we will know. So we have to act as normal as possible to have the chance to someday show how weird we are. Because everyone is weird.

Kevin was glaring at me. I had to act normal for his sake at this point, not mine. "So Kevin," I began, "How are you liking the new corner office? Big enough for you?" Violet caught Wanda's eye. Kevin gave me an appreciative nod. He launched into a well-rehearsed-but-not-well-enough-to-prevent-it-from-sounding-rehearsed speech about the pressures and responsibilities of his new job. "But the view," he said. He took a dramatic pause. "It's absolutely gorgeous." Violet practically swooned. "Sometimes I don't get any work done, It's so nice to look out." Both girls were loving it. I was long forgotten. The food came.

After a long meal, it was finally time to go. Kevin invited Wanda and I to join him and Violet for drinks at some place nearby. She made up some excuse, so I did too. I wasn't in the mood for anymore double-dating, and I certainly wasn't interested in third-wheeling. I patted Kevin on the back, nodded to Violet, and hesitated when I got to Wanda. She stuck out her tiny hand. Her nail polish was freshly painted maroon. It matched her dress.

"It was nice meeting you," she said. I took her hand and shook it firmly. It's funny, the lies we tell. I could already hear her complaining to Violet the next day: "He was so weird. All those corny jokes weren't even funny. You're lucky you met Kevin first."

"It was my pleasure," I said. I've always been a hypocrite. We all got to the door. I excused myself and went to the bathroom so that we wouldn't have to leave at the same time. The bathroom was impossibly fancy. They had scented soaps and warm towels for after you had done your business. There was an employee whose job was to stand at the front of the bathroom and nod at people as they came in. He wore a red button-down jacket and black pants. He had on a tall circular cap. He looked like one of the guards at Buckingham Palace. I imagined he was one, but at a crucial time he had moved, ruining the day of three tourists from Kansas who had come to see the guards not move. So he had been fired, and he had traveled to America in search of similar work. Unfortunately, the market for people who stand very still wasn't great, and this gig was the best he could do. I could see the sadness in his eyes as he greeted me with an almost imperceivable nod. His hair was cropped close and his face was pockmarked with acne scars.

"How's it going?" I asked, just to see if he could talk.

"Fine, sir, and you?" He had a nasally voice that drained the hope out of me. I didn't respond. I moved past him to the row of urinals. There was a man at the one closest to the stalls, and another standing with his feet spread wide at the urinal nearest to the door. The farthest stall was empty. Urinal etiquette demanded I take the stall over the middle urinal, to avoid the chance of social interaction in this wretched but beautiful place.

While I peed, I heard a loud crash. Someone had burst into the room. I heard a grunt and a man fall. I got on my knees (the floors were impeccable) and looked under the stall. A pair of heels walked slowly down the aisle, past the urinals. The depressed guard lay on the ground, not moving. The mystery woman kicked down the first door. She kept walking. She kicked down the second door. I was next. I was too scared to pull up my pants.

The door was kicked in. It swung open with a bang and bounced back. Wanda put out a hand and stopped it. She strutted into the stall and dragged me to my feet.

"I want you," she whispered. I was too stunned to say anything. "I wanted you as soon as I saw you." She pushed me onto the seat. I banged my ankle on the porcelain base. I brushed her hair out of her eyes and kissed her. She moaned. "I just had to have your--"

I shook my head, clearing my mind of the fantasy. I flushed the toilet with my shoe and zipped up. I washed my hands, sampling all the different scents. On the way out, I nodded at the guard, who I had taken to calling Chauncey. I apologized in my head for having him incapacitated to allow me to satiate my sexual desires. Horribly rude. I barely knew the man.

I was bored on the walk back. Walking always bored me. It was just me and my thoughts. No entertainment. I dug through my pockets and came up with a scrap of paper. It was Zoey's number. For what seemed like the hundredth time, I took out my phone to call her. I had a text message. I ignored it. I dialed the number. It rang as I walked. And rang. Finally, a robot told me that the number I was calling was not available, and prompted me to leave a message. I didn't know what to say. After a pause, I said who I was and why I was calling. I asked her to call me back at her earliest convenience, then chided myself for sounding like a middle-aged man calling a proctologist to inquire about his availability. I hung up the phone, already second-guessing my decision. I tried to think of a time when my mother setting me up with a girl had gone well. I realized she had never actually set me up with a girl before. My thoughts instead drifted to Brian's funeral...

It was the grayest day of my life. The trees were gray, the snow was gray, Amanda was gray. Everything was gray. The sun didn't come out once. I spent the whole day waiting for it to rain, for the weather to match the way I felt, but the rain wouldn't come. I couldn't cry. I was a mess. Amanda clutched my arm as we sat directly behind Brian's parents. I couldn't bear to face them. When his father spoke to me at the reception, his stern face wasn't even angry, it was just disappointed.

"You were his best friend." The admission seemed to cause him almost physical pain. I thanked him and looked for something to drink.

Earlier, I had sat there, and while looking around at all these people I didn't know, it became clear how little I really knew about Brian's life before NYU. We were college roommates turned best friends. The random pairing our freshman year had been willfully renewed the next year, and the next at the cheapest apartment close to campus we could find. We had upgraded, and Murph and Kevin joined us the next year, but I was never as close with them as I was with Brian.

For as much as I deferred to him, we were truly equals. He respected me. I respected him, and I loved him like a brother. Yet we so rarely spoke of the time before we met, of our childhoods. I had met only a handful of his high school friends, he had met even fewer of mine. These were the people that had come to his funeral. I could feel all of them blaming me-- the prolonged stares, the whispering that stopped as I approached and grew bolder as I left.

"They hate me," I whispered to Amanda, who had been strange all afternoon. She wore a black dress and a black hat. She looked too young to be at such a sad occasion. I imagined her at my funeral, wearing a veil and weeping silently as they lowered my lifeless body into its final resting place.

"You're being paranoid. A lot of these people probably don't even know who you are." This disheartened me. Their presumed hatred included a recognition of who I was: Brian Lewis' best friend. But if they didn't even know who I was, it cheapened our relationship: had Brian not talked about me to his old friends as I had him to mine?

The service ended. A few of us made our way out of the large funeral home, which had diminished the appearance of the size of the group there to say goodbye, out to the snow-covered cemetery for the burial. The snow crunched underneath my too-tight loafers as I reflected on the service. The rabbi had struggled to find the words to mourn Brian's death. He had died young, but it was his fault he had done so. None of the usual stuff would fit. The eulogies had been equally painful. I had not been asked to give one, which I resented and took as a sign of my guilt in the eyes of the family. After all, no one had spent more time with him over the past six years than I had. Hadn't I earned the right to say a few words about him?

Amanda clutched my arm as we walked. I wondered about her feelings. She had always enjoyed his company when he was around, but been highly critical of his drug use when he wasn't. She felt he was a bad influence on me. I didn't deny it, she was definitely right. If the NYU housing system hadn't spit us out as a match six years ago, I almost certainly wouldn't smoke, would drink less and burn less, and absolutely never would have tried cocaine. But I also would have missed out on some of the most amazing experiences and best stories of my life. I would be a different person. *Maybe that wouldn't be so bad*, the mean part of my psyche thought. I pushed those thoughts into a box with all the sadness and anger and guilt I felt, and I pushed that box as far down as I could. I knew one day that box would spring open and I would have to deal with them.

The rabbi stopped us by holding up a hand. Brian's father looked at me. I looked away. All of the work he had done to raise Brian to be a good man, to treat women right and to respect his elders, was for naught. Never mind that it hadn't worked that well, that Brian was a womanizing drugged-out failing actor, I had ruined his life's work of raising a son. He wrapped his arms around Brian's mother, who had started to sob. She was so much bigger than the last time I had seen her, almost three years ago. Her black dress was too tight, and the jacket she wore over it seemed ready to burst. Her sniffling cries drowned out the rabbi, a young man with long curly brown hair and those ear-things that very Jewish people have. I didn't know what they were called. I had systematically flushed out all my knowledge of Hebrew and Jewish culture as soon as the checks cleared from my Bar Mitzvah.

The wind blew, and I bristled in my suit. I had forgotten to wear an overcoat. Well, forgotten to own one, really. I had always borrowed Brian's when I needed one, but that seemed wrong to do in this case. I doubted he would have protested, but still. My peacoat didn't seem quite somber enough for the occasion. So I had figured I could be cold for a little while. But now I was regretting my poetic mind for suggesting any parallels between my discomfort and retribution for my actions. I put an arm around Amanda, not so much for her comfort as for the warmth of her body against mine. I felt movement in my pants, and was ashamed that I could feel and think in such a way while my best friend's corpse was ten feet away waiting to be buried in the snow.

A phone rang. An awkward looking grey-haired man apologized profusely. The rabbi looked at him. His hair was wild and his suit ill-fitting. He took out his phone. Brian's father looked at him. He seemed ready to answer the damn phone, when Brian's mother's sobs grew louder. He finally remembered where he was, and he silenced his phone. I wanted to break the thing into a thousand pieces and throw them in his face. Amanda stroked my arm. I glared at him. The rabbi continued speaking. A few muscular Mexican men stepped forward and began lowering Brian into the grave. This was it. I looked at the box that contained my best friend, and I still couldn't cry. I felt as if my inability to produce tears was betraying my best friend. I turned away. Amanda wrapped her arms around me from behind.

"It's okay," she whispered. I was grateful to her for lying. We both knew that nothing was okay, how could things be okay? I had contributed to the death of my best friend. Everyone who knew him would think of him as a cliche: the failed actor who overdosed on cocaine. All his traits, his complications and quirks, would be forgotten.

"We are all forgotten," I said back to her. She stared blankly at me. "Only a few people from any generation are truly remembered, and even they are forgotten eventually." Sympathy flashed across her face, it rearranged her features and caused her to squeeze me tighter. She said nothing.

Brian was in the ground now. His father stepped forward and, as per Jewish custom the rabbi explained, took a shovel and dumped the first pile of dirt on his grave. His face was impassive as he did so. I thought of what Brian had told me about his dad: how funny and corny he was, how much he loved his wife, how he had always been there for Brian. I thought how cruel it was that he had to do this, to bury the only son he would ever have. I took my place in the line. The world was silent. The only sounds were the chink as the shovel took a pile of dirt, and the muffled clump as the dirt and small pebbles landed on the mahogany coffin.

I got to the front of the line. How interesting, that the same mechanism we use to maintain order at McDonald's or the DMV is used to make sure everyone gets a turn to pour dirt on a young man. I took the shovel from a man I had never seen before. He was portly, in his early forties but looking much older. His yarmulke covered a bald spot. A flash of anger shot through me. Who was this man to take his turn before me? Surely he didn't know Brian like I knew Brian. I grabbed more forcefully than I should have. He stumbled a little, caught himself, and shot me a look. I looked back. He backed down, a habit of a lifetime of small conflicts with people that were stronger than him, physically and mentally.

I scooped a large pile of dirt onto my shovel, making sure it included the largest rock I could see. I rotated and glanced down into the grave. All eyes were on me. I still couldn't believe Brian was dead. It seemed like only a week ago we had gone to the gym, and passed hours pretending to exercise while scoping out girls and making fun of the muscle-bound men who could have crushed us if they wanted to. It seemed that way because it was that way. I looked at the rabbi. He gestured for me to dump dirt on my best friend. I resisted the urge to ask if he was late for his next funeral.

Amanda placed her hand on the small of my back. I sighed. I buried my best friend. The rock clunked against the wood. I was done.

My involvement in his life was over, but his involvement in mine would last forever. I resolved to never forget him.

I read a quote from someone somewhere that said something. I don't remember the exact words, but the gist of it was that you die twice: once when you actually die, and once when someone says your name for the last time. The saddest lives, I thought when I heard that, were those where the second death came first. I promised myself, as I stood there holding the shovel, prolonging a funeral that no one wanted to be at longer than they had to, that Brian's second death would come moments before my first, when I whispered his name on my deathbed. I placed the shovel in the dirt. I dropped my arms to my sides. I told myself I was being dramatic. I shot back that I didn't care. I had no response. Amanda bent over and I watched the curve of her back. She scooped a tiny pile of dirt and leaned as close to the coffin as she could. I crossed my arms. Her pile made a small pfff as it hit. It sounded like Brian snorting cocaine. As she straightened, I was struck by an intense desire to feel something else, anything other than the depression and hopelessness that had gripped me. She gently placed her hand on my tensed bicep and guided me away from the grave.

"I need you." I looked into her big blue eyes. She was on the verge of tears.

"I'm here for you, you know that." She hugged me. I whispered in her ear.

"No, I mean, like I need you. I have to feel something." She leaned back, her arms still around me, and searched my face. She found what she was looking for.

"Oh." She kissed me and I kissed back.

We fucked in the backseat of the rented Buick I had gotten to drive out to Westchester, where Brian was born and lived and would be for the rest of eternity. I lasted about forty-five seconds. We drove to the reception. Brian's father told me I was his son's best friend. I wanted to tell him he was Brian's father. I drank and drank and drank. I couldn't get drunk.

Afterwards, Kevin and Murph and I stood outside in the cold smoking cigarettes. We only had two, so we passed them around as if we were smoking weed. I wanted weed. Kevin wore what he always wore. I laughed in my head at the fact that he wore the same thing to pick up girls as he did to mourn the loss of a friend. Murph wore a grey suit.

"You don't have a black suit?" I was slightly offended by his cheapness. Brian would have bought a new suit for Murph's funeral. I pictured Brian in Murph's place.

"You're not really going to do this, are you?" Murph-Brian said. I frowned. What was happening?

"Do what?" Brian disappeared. Murph regarded me as if he were seeing me for the first time. I did my best to avoid the cliché of hallucinating my best friend.

"Criticize my outfit. No, I don't have a black suit. You always do this." I was confused. Was he really criticizing me? Today? On the day of my best friend's funeral?

"You can't be serious." Fuck him if he didn't feel sorry for me.

"What is your obsession with clothes man? You're always so obsessed with what you're wearing and what everyone else is wearing. It's Brian's funeral, for God's sakes, can't you take a day off?" I was taken aback. I tucked my hands into the pockets of my brand-new Armani suit and looked at Kevin. He was staring off into the distance.

"Are you really attacking me? My best friend just died." I waited for Murph to back down, to be ashamed. He didn't.

"Your best friend? Fine, yeah, he probably was. But do you not realize we were all friends with him? Don't you think we are all sad?" He dropped the cigarette on the ground. He put it out with one of his clearance-rack loafers.

"Well, I--"

"Or are you stuck so far inside your own mind that you think Brian only meant something to you? You don't have some exclusive right to be angry at the world for what happened. If anything, you have less of a right. You were there." Murph stopped. Kevin looked at him. The elephant in the room looked up when it heard its name called.

"Is that what this is about? You think it's my fault, don't you? Go ahead, tell me I'm wrong." I waited for them to say something. Murph bounced back and forth on the balls of his feet.

"I don't blame you for him overdosing. But you sat there for so many months while he did more and more cocaine and you didn't say anything."

"Neither did you!" I stepped towards Murph. Kevin stepped forward as if to grab me. I made an I'm Fine gesture with my hands. He relaxed.

"Yes we did, Zach." Kevin spoke softly. He wouldn't look at me. "We all tried to stop him. But he never listened to any of us. You're the only one who was ever able to change his mind. You're the only one who could be more stubborn than he was."

I thought back. How happy Brian was whenever I did coke with him. I realized that by joining him occasionally I had inadvertently validated all the other times he did it. I could see the logic he had used to rationalize his behavior. I had a good job, and I did coke. So it must have been fine for him to do coke, even if he did it in amounts that vastly exceeded anything I did. Amanda had come outside and walked over to us. I wondered how much she had heard.

"I, well," I stammered. What could I have said to that? Murph had made me realized that I was an integral part in the death of my best friend. I crossed my arms. I folded inside myself. I hunched over and wanted nothing more than to break down crying. Amanda put an arm around me and a hand on my chest. Kevin looked at Murph. They walked away. I turned and embraced Amanda.

When I got home from Westchester, I went to my closet. I tore out all my nice clothes and dumped them in a pile. I ripped my jacket off and tried to tear it. I couldn't. I pulled off the pants threw them into a corner. I kicked off my shoes. I wanted to scream, yell, to punch something, to feel pain. I didn't. I went to the kitchen. There was a half-bottle of bourbon left. Sitting in the rickety old chair that Amanda had always bugged me to replace and staring up at the peeling ceiling, I drank until I passed out.

The memory had taken me all the way back to my apartment. As I entered, I looked over at where the chair used to be. Amanda had won. It was one of the last things I did to please her before we broke up. In its place was a new, much nicer chair. It's white legs connected to a comfortable yet rigid light wooden base. It stuck out like a sore thumb at the small table which could be folded up and stored. The other two chairs were nowhere near as nice. But they were nicer than the old one, and thus they escaped Amanda's wrath. I took off my peacoat, but I was cold so I put on the grey shapeless hoodie I had bought a week or so after Brian's funeral. When I saw Murph for the first time since the funeral, about a month later, I was wearing that hoodie. His eyebrows raised, but he hadn't said anything, just passed me the blunt and continued telling some story about him and Jackie buying furniture together.

I looked in the fridge. I had no food, just empty six-packs and some old mustard. I took the three beers I could find and went to the other room. I plopped down on the recliner and drank them while I flipped through the channels. John Cusack appeared. He was talking to the camera. I hated that kind of thing. When the actors looked right at the camera and acknowledged they were in a movie. It was like the director was winking at the audience. I always felt like they were being condescending to me. I flipped the channel. Some alien movie. As the aliens land, drums pound and there is chanting. I laughed at how the music always sounded African whenever there were aliens. Good ole Hollywood racism. I flipped through the channels some more, passing by SportsCenter and some old white lady teaching people how to take frozen chicken and reheat it, finally getting to another movie. Seven Psychopaths. "Dream sequences are for fags," Colin Farrell told Christopher Walken. Same bullshit. A movie about a guy trying to make a movie. It just irritated me. I sucked on the bottle, then blew, trying to make a note. I failed. Amanda had always been good at doing that. I liked that she drank beer, a lot of girls don't. I reminded myself that I was over her.

I kept watching, even though they kept referencing that they were in a movie. It's pretentious, is what it is. It's like when an author interrupts his own narrative to give his thoughts on it. No one cares what you think, I wanted to tell them whenever they did. I know you think you're Vonnegut, but trust me, you're not.

I finished the beer well before the movie ended. I debated whether I cared enough to stay up and watch the end. I didn't. I turned it off as Sam Rockwell drove through the streets of LA. I undressed as I walked, tossing each article of clothing onto a random piece of furniture. I collapsed onto the bed and got under the blue bedspread I'd owned since sophomore year. I lay there. I couldn't sleep. I tossed and turned, replaying the dinner, every joke I made that fell flat, every comment Wanda made that irritated me. I was upset with Kevin for surprising me, especially with what it meant: he didn't think I had the balls to go on a blind date, so he had to spring one on me. I was more upset with myself for realizing he was probably right. I checked my phone to see if Zoey had called back without me noticing. She hadn't of course. I wondered what she looked like. Was it too much to ask for a smart, pretty girl that would love me? Besides Amanda? That was over. I amended the question. Was it too much to ask for a second chance?

Chapter 6

I lie in bed, unable to sleep. A purple light passes over me. I sit up and look towards the window. It is black at first, but then it morphs into something that can only be described as the absence of color. I look at the window, and see nothing beyond it. Strange music plays. I look around for the source. It is coming from inside my head. It sounds tribal, almost African.

All of a sudden, there is a loud crash. The ceiling peels back like a banana. I have a banana in my hands. It feels smushy. I throw it away and an orange appears in my hands. I decide to hold on to it. I look up and can see the sky. Or, I would see the sky, if there weren't a flying saucer right above me. I look at the silver circular ship and wonder if it uses Linux for its onboard computer. I then realize that my apartment is not on the top floor. I wonder what happened to the three stories above me.

I look around for Jeff Goldblum, but he is nowhere to be found. I try to get up, but my comforter has twisted itself around my feet and is restricting me from going anywhere. A hole appears in the ship above me. I start to sweat. No cover moves, nothing slides, there is no noise, a hole just appears. The music stops. A pinging noise repeats while a ladder slides smoothly down. It touches my floor. My heart beats quickly. Nothing happens for a moment. The walls of my apartment contract and expand, matching the pulse of my heart.

I note how far apart the rungs of the ladder are. A foot appears, then another. A being lowers itself (herself?) down the ladder. It does not look at me. When it lands, it pushes something on the ladder and the ladder retracts.

It turns towards me. It is not human, but it is distinctly feminine. I wonder if it has a name. *Xyla.* I don't hear anything and the creature does not move her (I'll go with "her," I figure) mouth. But I know that is her name. In fact, I notice that she does not have a mouth. Her face consists of a hole in what would be a human's forehead, and four oblong eyes. There are no pupils, only white spots.

Her body is difficult to describe. Some parts of her are simply not visible, though they must be there. *I reflect light that is beyond the visible spectrum*, she informs me telepathically. I assume that's what is happening. I start to speak, but she silences me by pointing to where her ears should be. There is nothing there. I wonder how to communicate, and then *You are doing just fine* appears in my mind's eye. I realize she can read my thoughts. She shimmers as she walks towards me.

I ask what she is doing here. She explains that her people would like me to come with them. I ask where. She does not respond. She explains that for generations her people have studied humans. They each take a turn picking who they will study. She has chosen me. I feel oddly flattered, but I don't want to go with her. Why? I ask, why should I go with you? She explains that in addition to telepathy, members of her race can see the future. It is easy, she adds, as a fourth dimensional being, to foresee things that will happen in three dimensions. My head starts to hurt. Why does that matter? *Because you end up alone*, she says. *Everything you fear comes true.*

* * *

A small pile of drool had collected on the edge of the bed where my head had been. My phone was ringing. It was Zoey. I tried to shake my head awake. I mentally prepared myself to sound intriguing yet accessible, and answered the phone.

"Hello?" Damn. I sounded way too eager.

"Is this Zach?" She knew it was me. Her voice was even, calm. Why couldn't I sound like that?

"Yes. Who is this?" I decided to match her false ignorance.

"It's Zoey." She waited. I waited. "You left me a message?" I got up from the bed and walked into the bathroom.

"Yes, right, sorry." I was too tired for this. I looked in the mirror. My hair was sticking up. I smoothed it down with my hand.

"You wanted to ask me something?" My hair sprung back up. I rubbed my eyes.

"Oh yeah, well, I mean, my mother wanted me to meet you, so I figured we could get coffee sometime. Or whatever." I had an eyelash stuck to my cheekbone. I picked it off.

"Or maybe we could go somewhere and eat a bunch of caramels." I laughed uneasily.

"What?" Just as I asked I got it. "My boy's wicked smaht." She laughed. "Alright, caramels it is."

"I was kidding." Her voice was warm. I tried to picture her, but there was too much I didn't know. What color was her hair? How did she hold the phone? I didn't even know where she was calling from. I knew how to play this game though.

"Well, I'm gonna hold you to it. We're getting caramels. You better pick the place though, 'cause I don't know anywhere you can sit down and eat just caramels." I went to the kitchen and got out a tea bag.

"Okay then, I'll have to do some research. When are you free?" I could hear voices in the background. Sirens. She was walking somewhere. Probably bored and decided to call me.

"I'll have to look." I took out a cup from the cabinet above the sink and looked in it. It was dirty. I put it in the sink and took out another. Dirty. I glared at my dishwasher. It had nothing to say for itself. I made a mental note to replace it.

"How about tomorrow night?" I regretted the words as soon as I said them. It sounded like I had nothing else going on. I found a cup that wasn't dirty.

"Hmmm, I think that will work. I'll look and let you know." I filled the cup with water and dropped the tea bag in it. I put it in the microwave and set the timer to a minute and a half. The microwave made a whirring sound and I didn't hear what she said.

"Sorry? I didn't catch that." I watched the cup rotate.

"I said I'll look and let you know." She sounded distracted.

"No I meant after that." I checked the clock. 9:48. I was running late, even for me.

"I didn't say anything." She took a sip of something. "Ow."

"What happened?" I went into the bathroom and put toothpaste on my toothbrush.

"My coffee's too hot. It burned my mouth." She had entered a building. The background noise went down considerably.

"Sugar, no cream?" I started brushing my teeth. I held the phone away from my mouth.

"Uh, cream, no sugar. What is that noise?" I spit out the toothpaste.

"Sorry, I was brushing my teeth. I'm late for work." I pulled my shirt off. It had pit stains. I grabbed a different one and pulled it on.

"What do you do?" I grabbed my Obey hoodie.

"No no no, I can't answer that." I picked up my keys. Guess I wasn't showering today.

"Why not?" She lowered her voice seductively. "Are you a spy?" I didn't respond. "Hello?"

"Sorry, I was trying to figure out how a spy would answer that question." She laughed. I liked her laugh, I decided. It came from her belly, not like a lot of other girls. She wasn't afraid to sound silly. I began to create an image of her based on almost nothing, and subsequently started to fall in love with that idealized woman.

"So why won't you answer?" She was intrigued. I hoped I sounded accessible.

"If I tell you now, we'll have nothing to discuss over caramels." I was only sort of kidding. Zoey laughed. We talked for a few more minutes about nothing. Eventually she said she had to go, she had gotten to her work. I didn't ask her what she did. We said goodbye. A warm feeling had started in my chest and spread throughout my body. I snapped my fingers a few times.

At work that day, I looked for places to sit and eat caramels. I didn't find many. My new assignment was to fix a fence on one of our many Farmville-like games. Apparently, sheep kept materializing on the wrong side of the fence and wreaking havoc. There was no way for users to shepherd them back through the fence because the fence had no holes in it. We were receiving a lot of complaints. I tried to picture the people who played these games, who got so frustrated at the transporting sheep that they would fill out a complaint and explain just how much gold they had lost. I was surprised none of them included the time they had wasted making their avatars chase little polygonal pixels in the shape of a sheep.

I opened the code. Yikes. It had very few comments and was poorly organized. I cursed whoever had written it and started combing through it, looking for the error. For once, I had an assignment that would take me all day.

Bob came over after lunch to make small talk and shoot the shit. We normally spent an hour or so discussing his feelings about the previous night's Knicks game. I'd worked there for almost two years, and he still hadn't grasped the fact that I wasn't a Knicks fan, and I knew almost nothing about basketball. He lamented the inability of Carmelo to pass out of a double-team, and I cut him off.

"I actually really have to focus on this, Bob." He seemed shocked. He straightened up and readjusted his fat red tie. It hung too far below his belt. His outfit, a white button-down and bland khakis, should have looked fine. But he had made just enough mistakes that combined to look ridiculous. In addition to wearing a tie that looked like it had been made for Drago, the buttons on his shirt were off by one and his fly was undone. He'd have been better off sticking to his usual stained polo.

"Course, I'm sorry, Zach, I should have asked." He ran a hand through his thinning hair. He was frazzled, distracted by something. I sighed.

"Are you alright, Bob?" The question hung in the air as we looked at each other. He opened and closed his mouth. He considered confiding in me. "Something you want to talk about besides Carmelo?" What had gotten into him? Bob was normally the fake-happiest one in the office, calling out everyone's name and having some sort of rapport with a majority of the office. Contrasted with me, who spoke to only a few people and knew even fewer names, he was a regular office-politician.

"Well, if you must know, I'm not that great." He rested his arm on the edge of my cubicle. I turned away from my monitor and faced him. "Yanni and I have separated. She took the kids." I gasped. Not dramatically, I was just surprised. Yanni and Bob had always been a strange couple, but a good couple. She was a quiet Chinese national who had moved here a year or so before she met Bob, a quiet American national who had never had a serious relationship before. I knew all this because Bob proceeded to tell me each of their life stories over the next hour while I alternated between trying to console him and attempting to extricate myself from the situation.

Eventually, he had pulled in another chair and was crying as he leaned on my shoulder. I awkwardly patted his bald spot while looking around for our boss. He was always around when I wanted to watch a video or duck out even earlier than normal, but when two of his employees spent an hour discussing marriage and crying, he was nowhere to be found.

Still, Bob's story unsettled me. As I finally convinced him to wipe his eyes and call Yanni, I thought about how great they had seemed together. I always considered marriage the finish line. You find the woman you love, settle down, get married, and are happy for the rest of your life. But I realized while that middle-aged man cried his eyes out that marriage is really the beginning. It's the start of a slog through babies, college funds, declining attractiveness, and money issues. There is no moment where the work is done. You have to fight for happiness your whole life. I leaned back in my wheelie-chair and looked at my monitor. The code I had been going through when Bob came over had been replaced by my screensaver. I had the one where you go through a never-ending maze, each turn leading to another set of choices. I wondered if I had the strength it took to be happy. My boss finally walked past and told me to get back to work. "I need that fence working by tomorrow."

It occurred to me that I might actually have to stay late for once. I redoubled my efforts and found the issue. I checked the author of the game and saw my name. It depressed me how unmemorable my own work was that it took me hours to recognize it. I fixed Earlier Zach's mistake. It seemed like that was all I had been doing recently.

Chapter 7

"So anti-humor is basically jokes that are funny because they aren't funny. Most of the setups are classic setups to jokes, and the punchlines are just statements that aren't funny." Zoey sat across from me, twisting her light brown hair around her long fingers. She leaned forward, yet seemed disinterested. *I'm losing her*, I thought.

"Okay..." She picked up a caramel, examined it, and popped it in. Her teeth were white and straight. That was the first thing I had noticed when the waiter had led her over to my table. I had left really early, thinking it would take me awhile to get all the way out to the restaurant, which was in the Bronx. She had told me over the phone that it was the only place in the whole city where you could sit and eat caramels. It was completely empty. We were the only two people eating there, and I had counted at least four workers wearing the dark brown uniforms. I thought they were supposed to be caramel-colored, but really they were shit-colored. I had pointed that out when Zoey first sat down, and she had laughed. But she hadn't laughed much since.

"Yeah, so one might go like this: 'a man walks into a bar.'" I paused. Zoey looked down at her phone and up at me. Her green eyes flickered in the dim lighting of the restaurant. The decor was downright bizarre. How does one decorate a caramel place? Apparently with lots and lots of modern art. Or as I call it, Paint Splattered in Random Ways. Painting after painting hung on the walls. The windows at the front were almost completely covered by the comic sans letters spelling out the restaurant's name. Chester's Caramels, it said. It had been established long ago in 2012. I figured it would last at most another month or two.

"His alcoholism is crippling his family." Zoey watched me. I wondered what features of mine she found notable. She didn't laugh. Not even a polite chuckle. I waited.

"Oh, is that it?" she asked, genuinely confused. She ate another caramel. I had lost my appetite. Everything was going poorly. I wanted to rewind, to start the date over. It was ridiculous, I decided, the way dating in our society works. You get an hour or two to convince some stranger that you just might be soul-mates.

"Yes." I admitted to my inabilities as a comic with regret. The conversation lagged. I wanted to ask her questions about herself, but a sense of failure had filled my stomach. I pushed my plate away.

"Are you done? Sorry, I'll hurry up." She had almost half her caramels left. She signaled to the waiter, who had hung within ten feet of us the entire meal, and asked him for the check. He was in his late fifties, with a shock of gray hair and very wrinkled skin. He had been exceedingly kind throughout the meal. I wanted to hit him. I wondered if he was Chester.

"Do you think he's Chester?" Zoey turned towards me conspiratorially. I laughed.

"I was just wondering that." A spark. The whole meal had been one of sparks and misses. There was something between us, I felt it. Or something could grow between us. We just needed another chance.

Chester brought over the check. He handed it over to Zoey. I took it from her. She resisted, but I pulled it away, thinking she was kidding. She frowned. I paid in cash and got up. She stood as well. I took her beige coat off the coat rack next to her and held it out. She paused, then turned around and let me put the coat on her. I could smell her perfume on the back of her neck as I did so. *It smells like lilacs*, I thought. A voice in my head pointed out that I didn't know what lilacs looked like, much less smelled like.

Outside, it was time to say our goodbyes. We had different trains to catch. I started to lean in for a hug, but stopped when she offered her hand. She wasn't wearing nail polish.

"It was nice meeting you," she said. Her voice was quiet. I hadn't lived up to her expectations. She hadn't lived up to mine, she was amazing in a way I hadn't expected. I took her hand and shook it briefly.

"You too," I said, unable to keep the sadness out of my voice.

"Are you alright?" She placed her hand on my arm. I considered the appropriate response. I barely knew this girl. This woman, I corrected myself. I noted again how tall she was, and was grateful that I was just a little taller. I could never date a woman taller than me. I had once, and I hated everything about it. Leaning up to kiss her, looking up to talk to her, the awkward angle it took to put my arm around her. I felt emasculated.

I knew the appropriate thing to do was to clear my throat and excuse myself. Explain that I was fine, that I had a nice time meeting her, and wait two or three days before calling her for another date. But I also knew that she would almost certainly decline if I did that.

In that moment of hesitation, I saw two paths diverging. One was me playing it safe, of waiting the requisite time and accepting rejection, of more nights spent preying on women with daddy issues, women with self-esteem issues, or girls with little experience. I saw the other path, a pitch, more like a plea, for another chance. An explanation of who I was and why I was. I found myself traversing the second path before I was even conscious of having made the choice.

"I just got out of a long-term relationship, and I haven't done first dates in a while, and I was never really good at them anyways. So I realize that you probably don't want to see me again, but I want to see you again. I think we have something here. If you give me another chance, if we could start over, have a date at an actual restaurant and eat actual food, maybe we could connect better. I just don't want this to be our only interaction when my mother was so adamant about how great you were and…" I trailed off. I had said all of this in one breath and now caught up on my oxygen intake. Zoey regarded me with a wary smile. I could see her considering me. I wondered again how she saw me, how she described me to her friends. He had a big nose and his eyebrows were too close together. His medium length black hair made me think he was afraid to take chances. I heard her slamming me, telling everyone about her horrible blind date and the plea I had made.

"Ok." She said it simply and with little trepidation.

"Okay? Okay what?" I was confused by her acquiescence. She brushed her hair out of her eyes. I shivered in the cold.

"Okay, we can have our second first date. And we can have it in a real restaurant." I buttoned my peacoat. She took out her phone and scrolled through something. "Are you free this Friday?"

"Yes." I didn't bother to look in my phone. I would make time if I had too. "Can I ask why?"

"I don't know. I guess it's sweet how much you care. And I didn't think this went as badly as you seem to have. The caramels were good. I think this place just might make it." I nodded. She started to walk away. I almost didn't catch what she said next. She tossed it over her shoulder like an afterthought.

"Besides, you're cute." I blushed. I hadn't blushed since high school. What was wrong with me? I watched her walk away. She looked back after ten or fifteen feet, and she seemed to be a little red too. It was probably from the cold. She smiled at me, I waved casually. I headed off in the other direction.

I walked around for a while, thinking. I realized after a few miles that I had missed the subway and was lost. I watched a few kids playing basketball at a park. They were around eight years old. One of them dribbled around all the others. White teeth shined out from under his dark skin and red lips. His face was an expression of pure joy. He ran towards the hoop and tossed the ball up. It missed, but he grabbed the rebound as all the other kids chased him. He ran and tossed the ball from the same spot. It hit off the bottom of the rim and another kid grabbed it. He tried to dribble but bounced it off his foot. The first kid won the race to the ball and stood there, bouncing it calmly. A breeze blew through the park. The chain-link nets tinkled in the wind. He ran around three kids, then threw the ball up from the same spot. It went in. I kept walking. My phone rang.

"Hello?"

"Hi Zach. I was just calling to check in with you about Friday." It was my mother. I was confused. For some reason I thought she was referring to Zoey. I pictured her round face, her upturned nose. God, she was too pretty for me.

"What? What's Friday?" I racked my brain for what she was talking about. She chuckled uneasily.

"Don't even joke like that. So, the movers and I should be getting into the city around--"

"Movers? What movers?" I remembered as I asked. My mother had decided she wanted to spend more time with me. No, that wasn't it. Edward had gotten promoted, and they were moving into the city so that he would have a shorter commute. I heard a sharp intake of breath as my mother prepared to chew me out.

"Zach-"

"Just kidding! Okay, I'll stop that joke. When are you getting in?" I had found the subway stop. I stood outside and searched for the quickest end to this conversation.

"Good, I was beginning to worry you hadn't been reading my emails. We'll be there around one or so, and I was hoping you could help me get settled in." I heard a door slam on the other end. Edward must have just gotten home. My mother laughed as he embraced her. I hoped that was what he was doing. I didn't want to picture anything else. I thought of my dad.

"Why can't Eddie do it?" I rubbed my nose with the back of my hand and felt a booger on it. I looked around and flicked it onto the ground.

"He has to work. And don't call him Eddie." I kicked the grated divider between the stairs down to the trains and the sidewalk.

"I have work too."

"Yeah, but can't you leave whenever? That's what you always say." I made a mental note to stop telling her anything related to my schedule.

"Okay, fine, I'll be there. I really have to go now, I'm about to get on the subway."

She told me the address and that she loved me. I said goodbye and hung up. The address was disturbingly close to my apartment. I rubbed my temples. I could feel a headache coming on.

I got very little work done that week. The dual specter of Zoey and my mother hung over me all week. I passed the time consoling Bob as his marriage fell apart while rating the songs in my iTunes. By Friday, I was up to U2 and Bob was hiring a divorce attorney. "It's a beautiful day," I told him. He didn't respond.

At around 2:00, I zipped up my Space Jam hoodie and headed over to the address my mother had given me. She was nowhere to be found. I leaned against the building and took out a cigarette. I reached into the pocket of my sweatshirt for my lighter and couldn't find it. I patted my front and back pockets and didn't have one either. I surveyed the people walking by, wondering which of them smoked. None of them looked foolish enough to spend ten dollars a day on killing themselves. I asked a big bald guy walking past if he had a lighter.

"Quit smoking a year ago. It's been 380 days since my last cigarette." He puffed out his chest and looked at my cigarette like a fat kid eyeing a Big Mac. He walked quickly away.

"Mazel tov," I said to the retreating figure. He was wearing white pants and a white flowing shirt. He looked like a sailor. I imagined him eating spinach with his wife and identical kids while they all glared at people outside smoking cigarettes.

I stood there with the unlit cigarette in my mouth. I thought it might be a sign from God that I should quit smoking. Then I remembered I didn't believe in God or signs. I looked around a little more desperately now. I saw two kids on the other side of the street. Freshman, I assumed, from the way they nervously looked around while passing a poorly crafted joint back and forth. I looked left and crossed the street. One of them saw me coming and gestured for the other one to throw down the joint. He did not. He was clearly the leader of the two, wearing a black peacoat and corduroy pants. He had a large head with a closely trimmed buzz-cut. I addressed him, ignoring his thinner, meeker counterpart.

"Either of you guys got a light?" I pointed to my cigarette. Alpha looked me over and said, "Brian, you wanna give him the lighter." Beta did as he was told. I looked at him while I lit my cigarette. He wore a blue puffy coat. It was unzipped and beneath it he was wearing a black shirt with a batman symbol on it. His shoes were neon-green. *Fucking hipster*, I thought. The flame kept going out before I could light my cigarette. I hunched over and cupped my hand around the lighter and the cigarette. I leaned down and finally managed to light it. I handed the lighter to Beta and turned around.

"You boys might want to consider spliffing that," I called as I walked across the street. A moving van was pulling out. My mother stood on the corner, impatiently tapping her foot. I went over to greet her. Without a word, she took the cigarette and threw it on the ground.

"C'mon, mom."

"It's good to see you too, sweetie." She opened her arms. I stepped into them. She hugged me. When I stepped back, she was holding the rest of the pack.

"Don't." She poured them on the ground, looking me in the eyes while she did so. "I get it, alright? You're welcome, by the way."

"Thank you for helping me move in. In return, I'm going to help you quit smoking."

"I can't wait." The corners of her mouth turned up. She was wearing lipstick that was too red for someone her age. Her pantsuit seemed too large.

"What are you dressed up for?" I bounced on the balls of my feet and looked around for a convenience store.

"It's not everyday you move to the Big Apple." She smiled and waved her arms in the air, to make sure I knew which Big Apple she was referring to.

"Don't call it that. Only tourists from China and Texas call it that." The movers came out and asked if we needed help unpacking the truck.

"Of course, that's what we hired you for." I looked at my mother, incredulous.

"No, actually, we can save a lot of money if we do it ourselves." She grinned at me and thanked the man. He didn't laugh. He had several day's growth of beard covering his dark face. Or maybe for him it was a day's growth. I stroked the space between my lips and chin where hair never grew. I wished I could grow a beard.

"Oh, honey, beards are gross anyways." My mother pinched my cheek. "We better get started." She picked out the largest box and strained to lift it. When she did, she handed it to me. She then found the smallest box and picked it up with one hand.

"Let's go. I'm on the eighth floor." I grunted. My back had already started to hurt.

A few hours later, I dropped the last box on the marble counter-top. It landed with a thud.

"Careful with that. That's the good china." My mother had performed her self-anointed role of supervisor admirably. I was covered in sweat and sore. I stiffly half-walked, half-crawled to the softest looking box and sat on it. I looked at my phone. I had an hour to get home, shower, and meet Zoey. I crawled towards the door.

"Where do you want to get dinner? I was thinking we could go to that place you were talking about. The Italian one." I had no recollec-tion of the conversation she was referring to.

"I can't eat with you, I have a date with Zoey." My mother bright-ened. She was so proud of setting me up with a girl.

"How is that going?" She took out her phone. She was one of the few people on the planet who still had a flip phone.

"It's alright." I searched for a way to end the conversation. "But it won't be if I'm late tonight." I headed out the door.

"Fine, I guess I'll have to get Edward to meet me somewhere." She didn't seem willing to let the conversation end. I shut the door behind me. My back twinged, I cried out in pain.

A painful twenty minutes later, I shuffled into my apartment. I searched for my bottle of Tylenol and took five. I showered sitting down. The hot water ran through my hair and down my face. I blew the water out.

As I gently toweled off, I looked in the mirror. I looked half-decent. I still needed a haircut though. I gently slipped into a pair of jeans and gently put on a pink polo. I flexed my arms and watched them move in the mirror. I smoothed my hair down, then mussed it up. Then I smoothed it a different way. After about five minutes, I found a look I liked. I ran my hands over my cheeks and felt the stubble. Just the right amount, I decided. I spun in a circle and snapped my fingers. My back exploded. I grabbed the sink with both hands and looked up at myself. I shook my head slowly and left the bathroom. I grabbed my peacoat and slipped it on. While waiting for the elevator, I noticed it had some stain on it. I rubbed it off with my nail, then flicked whatever it was on the ground.

While I walked to the Italian restaurant that I had picked out (Zoey had told me the onus was on me after she had managed to find the only caramel place in the Tri-state area for our first meeting), I rehearsed my opening lines. I rehearsed a few anecdotes that I could share. I rehearsed laughing at her spontaneous and relevant anecdotes that I was sure she would have regardless of the subject matter.

I saw her seated at a table in the corner when I got there. It was a small place, consisting of two "rooms" that were only separated by a frame that came down from the ceiling for a foot or so and then receded. She was seated in the back, near the bar. The bar had a white marble countertop and high black chairs crafted out of thin metal. The tables were a similar style, with thin twisting metal covered by burgundy tablecloths. She waved. Her hair was down, and she was wearing an olive blouse that was more revealing than what she had worn for caramels. Her jeans were a deep dark blue, almost black. I pretended not to see her, and had a waiter lead me over. He was a suave Italian man who spoke with a thick accent. It sounded too strong to be real. I figured it was supposed to contribute to the illusion that we were dining in Florence or Rome rather than SoHo. I thanked him and looked at Zoey. She frowned. I stuck out a hand.

"I'm Zach. It's nice to finally meet you." She didn't laugh.

"Oh, don't do that. You can come up with something better, can't you?" I sat down.

"Well, then. There goes all the lines I rehearsed." I sighed. She laughed.

"See? That was funny. Not that cheesy pretend this is our first date all over again stuff. You're funny when you stop thinking about what you say."

"Thank you? I think?" I took off my coat and folded it over the back of my chair.

"That was a compliment." She picked up the menu. "Let's get drinks. I've had a long day."

"I'll focus on the positive parts of it. And yeah, me too." I signaled over the waiter. I opened my mouth.

"Can we get a bottle of the house Pinot Grigio?" The words didn't come from me. Zoey smiled at me as the waiter wrote down her order and took the wine list. "I hope you don't mind, I've always wanted to do that."

"It's fine. But if we're smashing the patriarchy, you better pick up the check." She smiled wider.

"Well, I'm not completely opposed to chauvinism." I snorted. I looked over the menu.

"So if I'm not allowed to pretend this is our first date, I assume I can't ask again what you do for a living?" I looked at her over the edge of my menu.

"Well you wouldn't, except you never asked me that last time." She didn't look up from her menu.

"I didn't?" I put down the menu.

"It's okay, you were just concerned with making sure I understood anti-humor." I groaned and she laughed. "I'm a grad student at Columbia." I stood up.

"Well then, I think I better be going." Her eyebrows raised and her mouth opened.

"What, why?"

"Us NYU Bobcats don't mix with you highbrow types." I sat back down. We giggled. Our wine arrived. I poured us each a glass. "What are you studying?"

"Particle physics." I looked up. A little wine spilled on the table. She studied my reaction carefully.

"Wow, that's impressive. There aren't many women in physics, are there?"

"No, but there are probably more than there are in computer science." She took a sip of her wine. "Mmm, that's good. I love wine."

"Touché," I said. I racked my brain for what I remembered about particle physics from the one class I had taken sophomore year. "So, string theory?"

"Is a thing in physics, yes. Let's not do that, though."

"Do what?" I went back to the menu.

"I'll promise not to pretend to know how to program if you promise not to make me explain the universe to you." She leaned down and blew out the candles that were sitting on the table. I frowned.

"What did you do that for?" The waiter, I think his name was Marco, brought over fresh bread. I ripped a piece and Zoey passed me a pat of butter.

"I don't like the flame, it worries me." I spread the butter on the bread.

"Really?"

"There's a scenario I see playing out where the candle is knocked over, the tablecloth catches fire, and the whole place burns down in a fiery inferno. We escape, barely, but they expect us to pay for all the damages." She said all this quickly, then looked at me to see how I reacted. She was showing me her weird side way earlier than she was supposed to.

"That's all right, I'm paying for dinner, remember?" She smiled and I continued, "So that includes any fire-related charges." I bit into the warm bread. "You have to try this bread, it's the reason I come here."

"You bring all the girls here?" She took a piece of bread and bit into it.

"Just the ones my mother sets me up with. By the way, if we're sharing strange things we do in restaurants-"

"It's not strange to dislike fire."

"No, but it's strange to have a whole scene playing out in your head as the reason for disliking it."

"Fair enough, go ahead. What do you do? Eat with your hands? Order only appetizers?" She put down her menu and rested her head on her hands. She was interested, it seemed. "I'm interested."

"I like to sit facing the door." She faked being offended.

"Are you really asking me, a lady, to move?"

"I wasn't asking anything, I was just informing you of a preference I have. Now, if you were to take that information and choose to offer to switch seats with me, I wouldn't object..." I trailed off and snuck a peek at her cleavage. She noticed. I'm sure she did.

"Well, it just so happens that I also like to sit facing the door. I watch for assassins."

"Me too! Well, more like I watch for people I don't like so I can avoid them. But I imagine I wouldn't like assassins very much." I finished the bread and reached for another piece.

"I'll keep an eye out for you, how's that? If an assassin comes in looking for you, or if your mother were to have just walked in, I'd let you know."

"Jeez," I said, laughing, "I don't know which would be worse, an assassin or my mother." Zoey's eyes got wide. She shook her head.

"I certainly do hope you're kidding." My mother's voice was icy. I turned around. She was wearing a purple evening gown and had her arm linked with Edward's. That smug bastard nodded politely at me.

"Oh, Mom, what're you doing here?" She looked at me with derision.

"I decided, on my first night in a new city, to try a restaurant that my loving son who would never compare me to an assassin recommended. What're you doing here, and have you seen my son?"

"Look, Mom, it was a joke. I'm sorry." She looked at me for a few seconds longer. Her gray hair was pulled tight into a complex bun. I watched it while she watched me.

"Very well," she said. She called Marco over. "Bring us two chairs here, please."

"Are you serious, Mom? We're having a date." I looked at Zoey. She watched, amused.

"Well, now you're having a double date." She sat down next to Zoey. Edward sat down next to me and glanced at me apologetically. Asshole. He asked me to scooch over. I did so. I leaned against the light-blue walls and stared hopelessly at Zoey. She apparently found the whole thing hilarious. Marco handed my mother a menu. She ordered for all of us.

"Now then, how many times have you two seen each other?" She looked at Zoey.

"Well, uh, this is the second, but Zach wanted to redo our first date, so this is officially the first time we've met." She smiled at me. "It's going better, I think."

"Oh, honey, that's so stupid. Why would you be so lame?" My mother had turned her attention to me.

"I don't know, Mom, I guess I'm just a loser." It was middle school all over again. My mother was sitting me and my friends down to play board games all afternoon. We never went to my house again after that. Zoey chuckled at my sad face. I finished my wine and poured myself another glass.

"Slow down, honey." She redirected her attention back to Zoey. "You're over at Columbia, right?"

"Yes, and I really love it. The physics program is great." Zoey gesticulated with her hands as she talked, waving her bread around.

"Yes, it's a wonderful school. I wanted Zach to go there, but he didn't get in." I groaned.

"Um, well, it is difficult to get into." Zoey tried to soften the blows my mother was landing.

"If he had applied himself in high school…"

"Mom, I have a high paying job and am living in the greatest city in the world. What more do you want?"

"I-"

"Why are you doing this? Tearing me apart in front of this girl we barely know?" Zoey shushed me.

"Zach, please, I think it's adorable the way you two interact."

"You do?" I looked at her. Was she messing with me?

"Yes, I love to see how a son treats his mother.

"Just today, he walked out on me while I was talking."

"Is that what this is about? I had just finished moving all your stuff into your apartment so that you could save forty bucks."

"Yes, but you were so unhappy about it." She frowned at me. Our appetizer arrived. Calamari. My favorite. My mother didn't eat fish.

"Oh, Mom, I'm sorry. It's just I hurt my back, and I wanted to get ready for this." I gestured at Zoey and the restaurant.

"Everyone's sorry. Let's forget about it and eat." Edward spoke in a low baritone. He reached for a piece of squid.

"I'll drink to that." Zoey picked up her wine glass and clinked it against my empty one. I refilled my glass and poured some into glasses for my mother and Edward.

The food arrived rather quickly. We were the loudest table in the place. My mother and Zoey and I hit it off. Edward even chimed in occasionally with a comment that wasn't too annoying. Maybe he wasn't such an ignoramus after all.

When the check came, my mother took it. "I think we can get this one." I had never loved her more.

"Wait, in that case let me see a dessert menu." Zoey perked up and pretended to look for Marco.

"Don't do that, I know a place in the Bronx where we can all get caramels." I reached across the table and put my hand on her arm to get her to sit down. She looked at me and smiled. She had a filling in the very last tooth on the bottom right of her mouth. The imperfection only served to make her smile even prettier.

"Thank you," she said to my mother. She nodded at Edward too. He raised his glass in acknowledgement. "We'll get the next one." My heart fluttered. I had won. I earned a second date. Well, a third.

"Zoey, I think you might be drunk." My mother laughed as she put her hand on Zoey's arm.

"No, I'm just tipsy. Let's go mister." She looked at me. "We're going to kiss tonight." I laughed and Zoey laughed. Edward managed a chuckle. My mother beamed.

"She's direct, Zach. I told you that." Zoey and I got up and put on her coats. We said our goodbyes to my mother and my, well, stepfather. Two empty bottles of wine sat at our table. My mother and Edward each had half a glass left. They said they were going to stick around and finish it.

I walked her home. She leaned on me as we walked. "It's so cold." I shivered in agreement.

"Did you use your physics knowledge to figure that one out?" She laughed.

"I'm here." We stopped. We were standing very close to each other. She looked at me. I looked at her. Sirens went off. I turned just in time to see a dark figure running at me. I jumped back and he ran between me and Zoey. An overweight cop came running after him. He was panting heavily. His bushy mustache obscured his mouth. I could have sworn I saw flecks of donut crumbs in it.

He ran through us and stopped some fifteen feet away. He stood with his hands on his knees and took out a radio. He spoke into it, then turned and walked past us. Zoey and I watched him go silently. We turned as one to face each other. I started to say something.

"That was inter--" She silenced me with a kiss. Just as I leaned into it, she pulled back.

"Call me tomorrow?" She raised an eyebrow at me. "Don't do the whole two-day waiting thing."

"I don't play by the rules." She snickered. She kissed me quickly on the cheek and walked up the stairs to the front door. A pair of brass numbers indicated the street number. 68. She turned back to me. I waved.

"When I say call, I mean call. I don't want a text."

"So bossy. Very well, I shall call you tomorrow." She went inside. I stood there, triumphant.

Chapter 8

I walk through a desert. I am thirsty. I search for water. Brian watches me. I think it's Brian. He stays away, never close enough for me to make out his face. He drinks from a large bottle of water. There is lightning, then thunder. There is no rain. The sun comes out. It beats down on me. I wander in circles. I am crawling, desperate for a sip of anything. My lips are parched, my throat is so dry is has started to close. I lie in the sand and close my eyes.

I am hit by a wave of water. I open my eyes. I lie on a surfboard in the middle of an ocean. I see no land. Zoey is there, easily surfing and laughing in the whipping wind. She tosses me a water bottle and gestures for me to get up. She yells something. I can't hear her over the sound of the waves. I try to stand and fall. She laughs at me. Her hair is wet and it flies behind her. I stand again. I wobble, but do not fall. I look at Zoey. She screams. I turn and see a concrete wall coming towards me. I try to bail, but it is too late. I slam into the wall.

* * *

The pain in my back woke me up. I tried to roll over but it hurt too much. I groaned. I heard the faint sounds of traffic coming through the window. I looked at it and was grateful it was closed. I started to get up for work, then I realized it was a Saturday. I was like a little kid all over again. I checked my phone. It was only eight. I went back to sleep.

The pain in my back kept waking me up. I gave up at around eleven. I forced myself to get up and made a cup of tea. I put on pants while it spun around the microwave. I had filled the cup too much and had to carry it slowly back to bed. A few drops jumped the lip of the cup. They landed on my once white carpet. I thanked something (not God) that it hadn't landed on my bare feet. I looked down at my nails. They were getting long. My back twinged and I jumped. Tea landed on my foot and scalded me. I swore. My back swore. I reached the bed and sat down, placing the tea on my bedside table next to my phone and wallet. I examined my foot. I pulled the stretchy skin and prodded the toes. It didn't hurt anymore. My too-long nails reminded me of my too-long hair. I decided my activity for the day would be a haircut.

I picked my computer up from the ground gingerly. I slid back under the covers. I sat with my back against the wall and my laptop in my lap. That seemed right, somehow. I checked my email and had seven new messages. I didn't care about any of them, and left them unopened. I logged on to Facebook. I had no notifications or messages. But I did have a friend request from one Zoey Mclemore. *I wonder if she can rap*, I thought. I accepted the request and clicked over to her profile. 1,022 photos. We had one mutual friend. My mother.

I opened the most recent photo. Zoey in a coat and scarf, smiling with red cheeks. I went to the next one. Zoey with her friends, all dressed up and holding drinks. I went to the next one. Zoey and an older lady I took to be her mother. Zoey had her arm around her and was giving a gang sign. Her mother had a tough look and was holding up a peace sign. I laughed. Zoey was right, I decided, you can learn a lot about someone by watching them interact with their mother.

I started clicking quicker through the photos, going back in time. Zoey with red leaves all around her, Zoey at the beach, Zoey eating an ice cream, Zoey being held by another man, Zoey with her friends at a restaurant taking a picture of her food. I went back one. Who was that? He wasn't tagged in the photo. I looked for other pictures of him. I found several. I clicked on his name. Ryan Marcus. The ex-boyfriend. I compared myself to him. He was taller, from the looks of it. Blonder hair, bluer eyes, Hitler would have had no problem choosing between us. I hoped Zoey didn't have much in common with Hitler.

I looked at his education history. Damn, Columbia Law. Before that, Wesleyan. He worked for some law firm I had never heard of. She looked happy with him. I wondered what had gone wrong. I made a note not to ask her no matter how drunk I got.

I kept tabbing through photos. Zoey got younger and younger. Once I got to her prom pictures, I felt too creepy to continue. It bothered me because she was still attractive in those photos. I tried not to think about it. Our generation is the first that has problems like this. I can meet someone on the street and twenty minutes later be looking at pictures of them in elementary school. It's weird. I had very few pictures on my profile. I didn't like the idea of Zoey going through my photos as I had just done with hers.

The song "Hard in Da Paint" by Waka Flocka Flame started playing. I looked around, confused. It was coming from my phone. I answered it.

"Hello?"

"Hey, it's Kevin."

"Did you change my ringtone to Waka Flocka?" I ran my tongue over my teeth and realized I hadn't brushed them yet. Gross.

"Ha, no, I wish I had." I put my computer in the middle of the bed and got up.

"What's up?" I was confused. We rarely called each other. We each preferred the impersonality of texting. Brian had always insisted on calling, and I had always told him to text me.

"You haven't texted me back in a few days." I took the phone away from my ear and noticed that I had several texts from Kevin and Murph that I hadn't answered.

"Sorry, I've been busy. How's Violet?" I went into the bathroom. The tiles were cold against my bare feet.

"Who? Oh, uh, that's over." He didn't sound very broken up about it.

"What happened?" I couldn't find my toothbrush. I pivoted to look behind me and my back flared up. "Aargh."

"What? Are you alright?" He was impatient.

"Yeah, I messed up my back helping my mother move. She lives three blocks away now, can you believe that?"

"Jeez. She's uh, overbearing." There it was. The perfect word to describe her. It pretty much encapsulated the entirety of our relationship, some twenty-four years and nine months, and boiled it down to eleven letters. "Anyways, yeah, we slept together a few times-"

"Let me guess, nine times?" I gave up on finding my toothbrush and went to the kitchen to get a new one. I kept a bunch above my fridge because I was always losing them. Drunk Zach still wanted to have nice teeth, but he often didn't put his toothbrush back in the right place.

"Yeah. You know the rule. I didn't want a relationship, so it's over." Kevin believed that if you slept with a girl ten or more times, they'd become attached and want a relationship. So he almost always stopped talking to girls after the ninth time. I tried to remember his last long-term relationship. It was Marcy, I concluded, back in junior year. It had ended badly; she had cheated on him with someone, I couldn't remember who. But it was someone we knew. Kevin had spiraled into a depression. When I got dumped, I binge-drunk and did drugs. You know, the healthy way of dealing with emotion. When Kevin got dumped, he grew a patchy beard and tried to learn guitar. He would play these god-awful love songs for me and Brian. When he finished, I would tell him they sucked and Brian would tell him they had potential. After Marcy left him, he never let himself get close to a girl. He started making up all these rules for how girls had to act towards him if he was going to trust them, or for if they were dateable. Dateable. Whatever that meant. He was always jealous of me when I was with Amanda. Apparently she hit eleven out of the thirteen points on his most important checklist.

"Uh huh, and does she know that?" He also had a habit of breaking up with girls by cutting off contact until they got the message. I reached for the package of toothbrushes. My back got upset with me and pulled me back down. My fingertips grazed a toothbrush but couldn't take hold. I took out an icepack from the freezer instead and wrapped it in a paper towel, holding the phone to my ear with my shoulder.

"Well, she asked if I could hang out this weekend, and I told her I was busy." I slipped the pack under my shirt and held it against the left side of my back. I took the phone from its precarious position with my left hand and switched it to the other ear.

"You're a good person, Kev. Don't let anyone tell you differently." I made another attempt at the toothbrush. I failed. I decided I needed to change strategies.

"Whatever, look man, that's not why I called. We're going out tonight, and we want you to come with us. I haven't seen you in like a week."

"You miss me, baby? That's so sweet." I made my voice higher. I looked around for ideas. I had a baseball bat somewhere, Brian had left it here months ago and never taken it back. I went into the living room and opened the door to my closet.

"Fuck you, you coming tonight or what?" The smell of weed wafted over me. Apparently today was my lucky day. I couldn't see the bud, but I knew it was in there. I grabbed the bat, which was buried under a bag of golf clubs that I had forgotten I owned and my varsity jacket from lacrosse.

"Yeah, I guess. What're we doing?" I walked back to the kitchen.

"Murph had something planned. I'll text you later, we'll probably meet at Brad's."

"Of course we will," I said quietly. I reached up with the baseball bat and knocked the package of toothbrushes to the ground. Success. I bent over to get the package and ignored the signals the nerves in my back sent shooting up to my brain.

"Yeah, well, see you tonight." Kevin sounded uncomfortable.

"Wait, don't hang up." I got excited.

"What? What is it?"

"I love you."

"Oh, go fuck yourself." He hung up. I laughed. I went to the bathroom and put the ice pack down. I brushed my teeth. I stared into the mirror while I did so. I rubbed my head. Last day with this hair. I leaned in and spit out the murky paste. I washed out my mouth and looked at my cheeks. I could go one more day without shaving, I decided. I grabbed my razor and quickly shaved my mustache. Now I could definitely go one more day.

I returned to my comfortable perch and cursed. I went back to the bathroom and grabbed the ice pack. I returned once more and set up the ice pack to be held in place by the wall. I surfed reddit for twenty minutes or so, then put the ice pack back in the freezer. I decided to call Zoey while I searched for my treasure.

I grabbed my phone off the counter where I had left it. The screen was wet from where I had held it against my ear. I wiped the sweat away. I called Zoey. She picked up after one ring.

"Good to see you can follow orders."

"Yep, I pretty much do as I'm told." I opened the closet door and got down on my knees. "How are you?"

"Good, good. I met a cute guy last night for the second time and we smooched."

"Uh oh. Is he bigger than me?" I flipped over an old sweatshirt. Nothing.

"About the same. What're your feelings regarding stage productions?"

"What do you mean?" She talked funny sometimes. I also manipulated strings of letters in perhaps unorthodox ways as well when the fancy struck me.

"You know, actors, curtains, false narratives, that sort of thing. You like?"

"Yeah, sure." I dug through the junk. I had way too much crap in here. I began to worry the smell was an illusion, a combination of other smells that mixed in such a way as to taunt me. I wondered if "illusion" was the right word for talking about smells, or if there was a special word for false smells instead of false sights.

"Well then. Your enthusiasm is lacking. Would you like to go to a Broadway play with me tonight? My mom got me free tickets."

"First you friend me, then you ask me out? You certainly are direct. No societal norms will constrain you." I chuckled and lifted my old backpack. Bingo. There was about a gram in a little baggie in one of the pockets.

"Yeah, yeah, I'm a regular beacon of feministic pride and daring. You in?"

"Sounds delightful. When will you be picking me up? Should I wear a nice dress?"

"You can wear anything you want as long as it's not one of those hoodies your mother was going on about last night."

"Ah yes, my dress sense. Yet another way I have failed to meet her expectations."

"Whatever, Norman." I laughed.

"I hope we don't seem *that* dysfunctional." I held up the baggie to look at it. I stood up and slipped it in to my pocket. "Now it's my turn for questions."

"Very well, sir, fire away."

"How do you feel about certain illicit substances that the kids these days have been known to burn and inhale the vapors of?"

"I'm not going to smoke heroin with you, if that's what you're asking." I snickered. She laughed too. "But if you are offering me marijuana in exchange for theater tickets, I won't object." She pronounced the "j" in marijuana, so it sounded like "Mary-jay-wanna."

"Alright then, I just found a little digging around in my closet, so we are in luck."

"Why are you digging around in your closet? Oh no, are you like all the other NYU boys?"

"Very funny. I'll have to convince you tonight that I'm not."

"I don't know. You kind of kiss like a gay guy."

"What does that even mean?" She laughed and hung up. I went and lay back in bed. I pictured her lying in bed. I wondered if she was picturing me. I went into the bathroom and pulled off my shirt. I sucked my little belly in and flexed. I had a six-pack. Sort of. I took the baggie out of my pocket. Now I had to wait to smoke it. Oh well. I took off my jeans and turned on the shower. I took off my boxers and examined my penis. I considered shaving. But I hated shaving, and I didn't want her to think I was so presumptuous that I would shave for our third date. I imagined her naked. I started to get an erection. I looked at my penis in the mirror. I wished it were bigger. I wondered if there was any man who had a penis so large that he didn't ever wish that. I doubted it.

I got into the shower. I kept picturing Zoey. I realized I hadn't slept with a girl or done the other thing since I had been with... I wanted to say Becky? I chided myself for not even being able to remember the names of the girls I fucked. I tried to recite each of the women I had slept with. I gave up. My mind drifted back to Zoey. The water ran over me. I did the other thing.

Zoey came over at 6. I had hastily cleaned up before her arrival. Amanda had always criticized the mountain, so I pushed it into my closet. I wiped down the kitchen, tossed empty bottles into a bag and brought the bag out to the street, sprayed Febreeze as far as the eye could see, and generally did my best to upgrade my apartment from Filthy Bachelor Pad to Slightly Smelly Single Guy Suite. I texted Kevin to say I wouldn't make it, wherever we were going.

Zoey knocked on the door. "It's open," I yelled. I wasn't sure she had heard me. I got up and walked towards the door just as it opened. She was wearing a navy raincoat and purple boots. I glanced at the window. Apparently it was raining. Or she was insane. She shook her yellow umbrella out in the hall and then propped it up next to the door.

"It's really coming down out there." She gave me a hug.

"Really? The weather?" I smiled and took her coat.

"You know what would make for more interesting conversation?" She took out a lighter.

"A little weed?" I took out the baggie. I went into my bedroom to get my vaporizer. Zoey followed me, her head swiveling as she walked and observed.

"I was going to say a rapport established after years in a caring and committed relationship, but I guess weed will work fine too." I looked at her. She smiled somewhat nervously.

"I don't think you're supposed to be revealing how adorably quirky you are yet." I plugged the vaporizer into a socket and set it on the bed.

"I'm not?" She grinned at the words "adorably quirky." "What am I supposed to be doing?"

"Pretending to be perfectly normal until we like each other enough to reveal who we really are." I packed the vape.

"Well you certainly have a healthy view of how dating works." She sat on the bed. "Ooh, a water bed. Very nice."

"I like it. And that is how dating works." I was defensive. I knew how dating worked. I had lots of experience with girls.

"You think everyone just lies?" The vape had warmed up. I took a hit and passed it to her.

"I wouldn't say lies. I'd say presents an idealized version of themselves. And that ideal is based on movies and stuff." I looked her over. She was wearing a strapless aqua blue dress and matching heels. It looked expensive. I regretted not changing into nicer clothes before she had arrived. I wanted desperately to be wearing anything other than my faded purple t-shirt and old jeans.

"I'd like to live in movie world." She took a hit.

"I'll be right back." I grabbed a button-down and khakis and went into the bathroom. When I came back out, she had kicked off her heels and was lying on the bed. Her legs dangled in the air above her. She took another hit.

"It's definitely your turn now. This really hits."

"Yeah, my friend bought it for my birthday in college." I sat down next to her. She passed me the tube. I took a long hit, then another.

"Aww, how sweet." She grabbed a pillow and took a hit after I passed it back to her.

"Stop it. What were you saying earlier? About movie world?" I took a hit.

"Think about it. You never have to go to the bathroom, you rarely have to sleep. Everyone is pretty, and all your conversations are of the utmost importance. Plus, almost everyone who's nice gets a happy ending." She took a hit and coughed. I laughed. She looked hurt. Then she laughed.

"Well," I said, taking the whip from her. "I just want the happy ending." I breathed in from the mouth piece. She giggled. "Not like that. I didn't mean it, y'no."

"I know what you mean." We sat in silence for a few minutes, passing the whip back and forth.

"What do you call this?" She asked. She held up the whip. "I never really vape."

"It's called the whip."

"Oh."

We sat there. It wasn't awkward, but I felt like it should be. I wanted to talk about something. I didn't want her to get bored.

"When do we have to leave?"

"It starts at... 7:30 I think. So, I don't know, 7:00?" She looked at me. Her eyes were red. I laughed.

"Don't ask me, you're the one running the show tonight."

"No that's my mother." She laughed at that. I didn't get it. "Very well, good sir. We shall depart at 7."

"Fantastic." I lay down next to her on my stomach. I didn't care if my clothes got wrinkled, I decided.

"Here's the whip." She held it out to me. I took a hit while she held it. She laughed. I leaned back and turned towards her. She turned towards me.

"Thank you."

"You know, we're doing this all wrong." She took a hit. "I think it's kicked."

"I'll repack it." I started to get up. She put her hand on my shoulder.

"I'm good." I stopped moving. She left her arm there.

"Whaddyou mean, all wrong?" I looked in her green eyes.

"Well, think about it." She sat up. I did too, looking at her intently. And contently. "I met your parents on the second date."

"Mom and step-dad." I corrected her.

"Whatever. You're going to meet my mother, and maybe my dad, tonight.'

"I am? I didn't know they'd be there." My eyes widened. I started to get nervous.

"Relax, they'll love you. And yes, my mother is directing the musical, of course she'll be there. My dad probably will too."

"Oh, yippee." I lay back down. I grabbed the whip and took a hit. It really was kicked.

"So there's that. And think about our third date."

"This one, you mean?" She laughed and lay back down. My face was inches from her face.

"Yes, silly, this one." I flicked her nose with my pointer finger. Her skin was warm. I don't know why it wouldn't be. I imagined her as a zombie, her skin cold and clammy, shreds of flesh in between her teeth and the light going out from her green eyes. Patches of hair would fall out as she chased me maniacally around my apartment, limping on a broken foot and a thigh with large chunks of muscle missing. "We're starting in your apartment, lying on your bed. We're supposed to end here, not leave here."

"Well-"

"Omigod, just kiss me." I kissed her. She rolled on top of me. I cried out in agony. "What? What did I do?"

"It's not you, it's me."

"Wow, cliché alert."

"No, I mean…" I rolled away from her and put one hand on my back. I tried to massage the pain away. "Yesterday my mom moved into the city, and instead of paying for large Latin men to carry her things in, she decided to save a few bucks and use slave labor. Me."

"And you messed up your back? Why didn't you tell her?" She moved my hand and massaged my back. The tension left. I relaxed.

"She always freaks out when I get hurt. If she thought it was her fault, she'd have been even more upset." I hated myself as I was saying it. I knew that reasoning would make me look good, make Zoey like me more. I felt like a fraud who was manipulating her, even if it was true. I thought she must know I would know how she would react and be upset. She didn't.

"That is so sweet." She continued massaging by back. "Does that feel better?"

"Yeah, it went away almost immediately, I was just enjoying the massage." I laughed. She tittered, but also punched me lightly on the arm.

"What was that for?"

"For taking advantage of my kindness." She looked at her iPhone. "Now, come on, we've gotta leave." I got up and smoothed down my shirt.

"Okay, let's go. I hope you know the way." She sat up and reached for her heels. I bent down and passed them to her.

"Me too." She put on her shoes and took the hand I offered her. While she put on her coat I went and found my rain jacket.

"Hurry up," she called. "This whole place smells like it was just febreezed."

We walked slowly down Broadway. Cars honked all around us. I held her hand. We interlaced our fingers. As we crossed from 47th to 48th street, a cab almost hit us. I jumped back and pulled her with me.

"I'd hate driving in this city," I said, staring after the cab.

"Really? Why?" She seemed to genuinely not get why. I handed her eye drops for her eyes, which looked as if she had been up for weeks planning a series of complicated and risky murders.

"Because I'd always be afraid I'd cut someone off and get honked at, or people would cut me off and irritate me, or I'd get hit by another car and die." She put a few drops in each eye.

"Better?"

"Much." I took the bottle back.

"How come you have those if your eyes don't get red." She stated it more than asked me.

"I used to always smoke with my friend whose eyes got really red. I wanted him to take the drops so people wouldn't know. He didn't care." She turned left and pulled me with her. An old lady with white hair looked at me. The rain poured down. I moved closer to Zoey, ostensibly to get farther under her yellow umbrella. Our shoulders ricocheted off each other. She turned and looked at me. Her eyes were half closed. Or half open, I figured, depending on if I was an optimist or a pessimist.

"Why 'used' to? You don't smoke with him anymore?" I pictured Brian's smiling face.

"No, he's uh, dead." Her smile vanished. Brian vanished from my mind.

"Oh, I'm sorry, I didn't know." We walked in silence for a little, our shoulders touching and separating repeatedly. I looked at all the bright lights and wondered when we were going to be there. I checked my phone, 7:24.

"If I was driving, I wouldn't mind if you cut me off." She said this simply, then her eyes flickered over to me to check if I was listening. I was, sort of. "I like being cut off."

I bit. "What? How could you like being cut off?" She laughed. I chortled.

"I like getting to use the horn. I'd give you the horn when you cut me off." I looked at her. She smiled at me and bit her lip.

"You," I began, "are very weird." She frowned. I kissed her. She pulled back.

"We're here." I straightened up and peered through the rain at the sign. *Fins Heureuses*.

"I've never heard of this play. Is it any good?" She gave our tickets to a large Asian man in a red jacket and hat.

"I don't know, but either way we are going to tell my mother afterwards that it was amazing." We walked down a well-lit hallway. It had the standard red carpeting and other warm colors. There were posters for various plays and musicals on the walls. I had never heard of most of them. I chuckled as we made our way down into the front rows. An older lady led the way. She had white-blond hair and a soft smile.

"Enjoy the show." She waved and was off to escort more theatergoers to their seats.

"I feel so cultured." Zoey whispered in my ear. Her breath tickled. I slouched away.

"I just hope it has a happy ending." Zoey looked at me for a second.

"I guess you don't speak French, do you?"

"Nope. I speak American, and I'm not even good at hat. I mean that. I mean it." I shook my tongue as if that would help me speak better. Zoey giggled.

The curtain raised. A petite man dramatically produced a diamond ring. He perched on one knee and proffered it to a beautiful black woman wearing a dark blue dress and black heels. She squealed in delight, and they kissed. The curtain dropped.

The play was… interesting. It was also very long. I spent the whole time alternating between laughing at the not funny parts and wanting to check my phone to see the time. It couldn't go more than two hours, I told myself.

"It can't go more than three hours, right?" I asked Zoey after the intermission took place two hours after we had first sat down. It was interesting, sure. It was about what happens after the proposal, after the happy ending of most plays. The problems people go through even when they are married to the love of their life. I had never really considered that. Ever since Randy had explained the two stages, I had convinced myself the only hard part was the time spent in between the stages, the intermission if you will.

"You don't like it?" Zoey frowned, then giggled. I looked at her, laughing with a sad face, and something stirred inside me. I felt close to her, something that I had only ever felt with two people, Brian and Amanda. But more than that, I felt I could let my guard down, something I had only ever felt with Brian.

"No, I do, I'm just curious." She smiled and squeezed my arm. I wondered what she was thinking.

Afterwards, we went backstage to meet her mother. As we approached an older lady who looked important, with heels and a black suit on, I stepped forward.

"That was amazing," I said. I stuck out a hand to introduce myself. Zoey crept up behind me and whispered in my ear.

"That is not my mother." I straightened up, embarrassed. The woman laughed and walked away.

We eventually tracked down her mother. You know that cliché about it being obvious where a daughter's beauty came from? That didn't apply at all in Zoey's case. Her mother had platinum blond hair, brown eyes, and cheeks so tight I thought for the first five minutes she might be sucking on a lozenge. She was pretty, I supposed, but she looked nothing like Zoey. We chit-chatted for a while, then she adopted a stern look.

"What are your intentions with my daughter?" Zoey giggled.

"Mom, don't do this now. It's our third date."

"I'm going to marry your daughter," I said with a straight face. "And we are going to have beautiful children." Zoey looked at me for some sign I was joking. I stayed serious and didn't look at her.

"I like him." Her mother said to Zoey, and turned to me. She smiled. "You hurt her, and I'll hurt you. Understood?"

I nodded solemnly. I was afraid I would hurt her. I didn't want to, but I was afraid we'd end up like Amanda and I had, former best friends who no longer spoke to each other. We said our goodbyes, and Zoey clutched my arm with both of hers as we walked.

"Someone is getting laid tonight." She laughed and winked at me. I chuckled. I was still high.

"By golly, I sure hope it's me. Well, not just me." She tittered and I removed my arm from her grasp and draped it over her.

We had sex that night. A lot of it. As soon as we were in the door she was on me, kissing all down my neck and taking off my coat. She flung it on the ground.

"There's no need to make a mess," I told her. I took off her coat and threw it on the couch. "But then again, why not?" She chuckled as I kissed her. We didn't even make it to the bedroom the first time. I didn't last long.

"Sorry," I panted heavily. "Increased sensitivity and all that."

"It's okay, we'll have plenty of more tries." She bit my neck and got up. I watched her naked cheeks sway as she walked into the kitchen. "Let me get you some orange juice. You go wherever you keep all your condoms and bring back all of them." I got up and practically ran to the bathroom. I pulled off the condom we had just used that I kept in my raincoat. I threw it in the toilet and flushed. I went under the sink and grabbed a roll of condoms.

I walked into the bedroom. Zoey poked her head through the door. She was holding a glass of orange juice. I drank it while she wrapped herself around me. As soon as I finished she spun me around and mounted me.

I had never felt like Amanda withheld sex from me, or that it was a chore for her. But once was always enough for her, while Zoey was insatiable. We'd finish, I'd go to the bathroom, dispose of the condom, and stumble back to the bed. My back was on fire, but I didn't care. We'd cuddle for a little bit, then she'd look up at me, or I'd tilt her chin up to me with my finger, and we'd be off again.

Zoey left around three the next day. I was sweaty, exhausted, hungry, and weak in the hips. My penis was a shriveled peanut. I looked at it as she gathered her things and prepared to leave. She came back to the bed and kissed me fiercely.

"Before you go, I want to make something clear to you."

"If you tell me you're not looking for a relationship now I'll cut off that tiny salami." I looked down in shame.

"He's tired, all right?" She laughed. She sat down and stroked my hair.

"I'm still kind of messed up from Brian dying and Amanda leaving me."

"Brian's the friend who died?" She put her hand on my cheek and turned me to look at her.

"Yes. So if I act weird, or like a douche, or whatever, I want you to know it's not you, I'm just kind of fucked up right now." She laughed and got up. I stood up and grabbed a pair of boxers. I got into them, almost tripping.

"Nice try." She looked at me sternly. "You don't get some sort of get out of jail free pass because you just broke up with a girl. If you treat me like shit, my large gay friends will have a word with you."

"Scary." I laughed. She was weird. So was I. I kissed her good bye. She grabbed her umbrella and went to the door. Just as she opened it, she said to me, "Do I need to leave something here, or will I be invited back?"

"I don't know, might want to leave something just to be safe. Your bra, maybe." I smiled so she knew I was kidding. She waved and left. I stood there, half-naked, smiling, as happy as I had been in a long time. I went to the kitchen. My khakis from the night before were hanging off the refrigerator. I dug through them for my phone. Kevin had called again. I called back.

"Thanks for bailing on us last night." He sounded pissy. He hated Sundays, I knew. There was never a reason for a failed Christian like him to wear a suit. I dragged the khakis back into the bedroom. I opened the closet and tossed them onto the mountain. A few articles spilled out onto the floor.

"Sorry man. But I've met someone, and she's amazing." My voice seemed higher than normal.

"Oh. Well that's great. Is it that girl that your mom knows?" He seemed happy to hear the reason I hadn't seen him in so long. I absentmindedly tossed the clothes back into the closet one at a time and made no effort to stop the pieces that fell to the floor and replaced them.

"Yeah, her name's Zoey. She just left." I was unable to hide my excitement. I always told myself I wouldn't brag, but I always did. But this wasn't supposed to be a "I just had sex" brag, it was more of a "the love of my life may have just walked out that door," kind of brag.

"She's been there since last night. Jesus man, that's insane. How's the back?" Kevin didn't see it that way apparently. I twisted back and forth.

"Surprisingly better." I gave up on reassembling the mountain and shut the closet door. I grabbed a stress ball that was lying on the ground and lay back on the bed.

"You know what they say: sex heals all wounds." I laughed. I tossed the ball straight up in the air and caught it. I squeezed the purple foam and read the writing on it. It was from NYU.

"Yeah…" I wasn't sure what to say.

"So when do I get to meet her?" A good question. Did I want her to meet my friends yet? Would they judge me for dating her so soon after Amanda, or think she was just a rebound? More important, was she just a rebound? I didn't think so. I pictured her looking up at me while she kissed my belly button. My shriveled member tried to rise, but gave up.

"Uhh, soon. Yeah, soon." I said I was starving and had to go. I had some cold pizza in the fridge, a rarity.

"Okay man. Don't forget about us." He hung up. I laughed while looking at the phone. I would never do that. Brothers before whores and all that jazz.

Chapter 9

But he didn't meet her soon. She was so busy I barely got to see her, let alone take her around to meet my friends. We spent as much time as possible together, but she was nearing graduation and had to apply for jobs as well as do all her work for her classes. She was always so frazzled when I saw her. Sex was the only thing that relaxed her, she claimed. I wasn't going to argue. Weeks passed, and before I knew it we had been dating for three months. The time passed quickly, I had thrown myself into a new game at work. It was like a dolphin version of Farmville. Users would play as different dolphins and interact. They could buy coral, which served as currency in the dolphin society. Bob left the company, and I was promoted to his old position. I did the same thing, I just had the word "Senior" in front of my title. I realized one day that I was among the three oldest programmers there. I checked my hair everyday for signs of gray or balding, and each day I resolved to get a haircut. I never quite found the time. The irrational part of me feared Zoey wouldn't like my haircut, and would leave me for a strapping young Puerto Rican pool boy. I made a concerted effort to see my friends whenever Zoey was busy. We still went to bars and smoked pot together, but something was different. I wasn't as interested. I'd say it was because I was taken, but I had gone to bars when I was with Amanda and simply enjoyed the scenery. I thought it might be a sign I was moving from stage one to stage two. I asked Randy if he agreed.

"Stage two? What are you talking about?"

"Never mind." I reconsidered the wisdom of measuring my life's progress according to the advice of a stoner who couldn't even remember advising me.

Every girl I saw reminded me of Zoey. I'd catch a whiff of perfume and be convinced she had come to surprise me. I'd spin around and see a bunch of college freshmen and be disappointed. One of them would bite her lip or fiddle with her hair and I'd see Zoey performing the same maneuver. I would sit and watch my friends strike out with girls. Picking up chicks is like hitting a baseball: the best players in the world are out of luck seventy percent of the time. My friends were not the best players in the world; Kevin was at best a promising double-a prospect. Randy and Louie were like the superstars of slow-pitch softball who lament the mysterious knee injury that ended their promising careers while drowning beer after beer and citing obscure rules that no one cares enough about to look up.

My friends jokingly would doubt Zoey's existence. I thought the newfound cleanliness of my apartment would serve as evidence that there was some new woman in my life. If I refused to wingman for them, they'd ask if Zoey was sitting next to me. I'd laugh, but longingly glance to my right or left in the off chance she'd appeared in the last ten seconds without me noticing.

"Enough's enough." Kevin yelled to me over the loud rock music at Josie's one night. He had two drinks with him. I took one without asking. We'd been there a few hours. Louie had left with some girl, who was most generously described as "having a nice personality." Randy and Murph were floating around somewhere, prowling around like a pride of lions searching for wounded gazelles. I had sat in the same spot all night, downing beer after beer and glancing at my phone hoping Zoey had finished her work and would be joining us. I thought sadly of all the other grad students who got to spend so much time with her working on various projects in close quarters. I considered quitting my job and pursuing a career in physics. The still-sober part of my brain pointed out a few of the many flaws in that plan, most notably the level of stalkertude I'd reach if I did so.

"When am I going to meet this woman?" Kevin sat down next to me.

"I don't know, she graduates in a few days, and she hears back from a few places she applied to, tomorrow." I selfishly wished she wouldn't get the job she wanted, so we could have consolation sex. I then realized celebration sex was probably better, and knocked on the wooden table in front of me. Kevin looked at my hands, deep in thought.

"I got it!" He had undone the top two buttons of his light purple button-down and it was half untucked. I pointed out the issue, and he rectified it by pulling out the other half.

"What did you get?" I asked after thirty seconds of silence while I waited for him to continue. I sipped the drink I had taken from him. It was a deep blue. It tasted like lime and vodka. Mainly like vodka. "What is this?"

"It's called an *adios, motherfucker.*" *How classy*, I thought to myself. "We should have a party. I'm gonna throw you guys a party." I knew he would decide in a few days, if he even remembered this conversation, that it was best to throw said party at my apartment.

"What for?" I took another sip, then decided I didn't feel like saying goodbye to any Oedipus wannabes quite yet, and placed the drink on the fake wooden table.

"It can be a celebration of your birthday, Zoey graduating and getting a job, and a chance for us all to meet her." I considered it. My birthday was the next weekend. I was turning twenty-five. I shuddered at the idea that I had been on this planet for a quarter of a century.

"It's a good thing I'm not a musician." Kevin frowned at me, confused. "I'd only have a few years left." He didn't get it. Zoey would have.

"Is that a yes?" I thought about all my friends meeting Zoey. It was time, I decided. I grabbed the glass and raised it.

"Let's do it." Kevin cheered. Randy came and sat down. "Where's Murph?" He nodded to the corner, where Murph was intertwined with a purple-haired girl who, I noted with some foreboding, had spikes on her belt and boots. "Excellent selection," I commented. We all laughed. We drank the night away. They all got laid. I checked my phone when I got home. Nothing.

* * *

"My friends are throwing us a party." Zoey rolled over in bed to face me. We were at my place. I had only been to her apartment twice. She preferred coming here. I didn't mind.

"Oh yeah, for what?" She didn't open her eyes. I had almost sexed her to sleep. I was proud.

"To celebrate you graduating and my birthday, but it's mainly just an excuse to come over and drink at my apartment. Plus, they don't believe you are real." She opened her eyes.

"So many questions. Were you planning on telling me your birthday was coming up? When is it?" She hit my chest playfully.

"It's Saturday. I didn't really know how to bring it up. I was hoping you'd see on Facebook." She started playing with my chest hair.

"I love how well we communicate. Now, about them not believing I'm real? Do you have a habit of getting Te'o'd?" I laughed.

"No, Lenny, I don't." She rested her head on my chest, I put a hand on her head and stroked her hair.

"Lastly, why will they throw a party at your apartment if it's for you?" She walked her fingers down towards my waist.

"It's what Kevin always does. He claims it'll be at his place, then he calls the day before to say the landlord won't let him or some other such nonsense." Her fingers completed their journey. I kissed the top of her head. We didn't talk again about anything but positions and angles for an hour.

"Do you feel old?" she asked me later that day. She was washing her hands in the sink. "No, not really. After all, I'm nowhere near as old as you." She had turned twenty-five the week before I met her. She laughed. "Well, my elderly wisdom tells me you will start to feel old about a day or two after you turn twenty-five. Right about when you realize you are closer to thirty than twenty." I was quiet. She was right. I was an adult now. I shuddered and turned on the television. Spongebob was on. I sat down to watch. Zoey grabbed an apple and sat on the recliner. We watched mindlessly, laughing at the jokes for kids more than the ones for adults.

* * *

I only saw Zoey one more time before my birthday. She showed up at 1:00 in the morning on Tuesday, to celebrate her getting a job with some defense company. We fucked to commemorate her new-found love of warfare and murder. Kevin called on Thursday to say he was so so sorry, but could we possibly have the party on Saturday at my place? I said sure and hung up.

The day of, I woke up and went out to buy beer. Kevin had given me a couple hundred in cash he had collected from Murph, Randy, and Louie. I suspected my mother had chipped in as well, because she called to inform me she had a lovely conversation with Kevin, and to remind me of the dangers of binge drinking.

"Oh, and happy birthday," she said right before she hung up. Randy texted me to say he had a very special birthday present for me. I wondered if it was acid or peyote. I knew it wouldn't be cocaine. I realized with a start that I hadn't thought about Brian in a few days. It was the first time since his death that I hadn't thought of him at least once in a day. I wished he would have been able to be there, to meet Zoey. I was becoming more and more sure that I had moved into stage two. I imagined proposing to Zoey. I went out to get a slice of pizza for lunch.

As I walked, I examined my fellow inhabitants of the city. I had made it here, I realized. I had a good job and a great girlfriend. My friends were throwing me a party. I could make it anywhere, I postulated, but I didn't want to make it anywhere else. I breathed in that unique smell of urine, body odor, and halal food that you can only find in a big city. I considered the usefulness of the oxford comma.

I passed the street vendors. Fake gucci, faker watches, and fakest smiles. The middle aged Muslim men jostled with one another for position as I walked past. I shook my head at each of them. I decided to walk to Chinatown for some dumplings. When I reached Canal St, I paused and surveyed the crowd. So many people, each of them the star of their own stories. They were all weird, all complex, all insane individuals with wants and desires and hopes and dreams and secrets and shame. I entered the restaurant. It was a hole-in-the-wall. There were no tables, just a line to order and a line to pick up your food. I waited patiently. The woman in front of me couldn't decide. She had short bushy black hair and was wearing an army jacket. She scratched her head.

"What you want?" A short young Chinese man stood on the other side of the counter. I wondered about his life. Get up, spend all day serving tourists and businessmen, clean up and go home to get ready to do it all again the next day. His impatience was understandable. I made sure to have my order ready. I rehearsed saying it as the woman in front of me stuttered. I placed my order calmly and the man nodded at me. I wondered if he was married, if he was dating, or if he was all alone. While I waited for my food I looked at each of the other patrons, and at all of the staff. How many of them were married? How many of them hadn't found anyone? Worse, how many of them had married the wrong person? An old Chinese lady handed me my food in a plastic bag. I grabbed a spork from the cup on the counter. I asked for extra soy sauce. She threw me two packets. They bounced off my stomach and fell into the bag.

I ate as I walked, careful not to spill any on my beige cardigan. My sense of style had returned, my desire to dress nicely for Zoey had cost me quite a bit of my promotion bonus money as I reacquired a nice wardrobe. The old one had taken me five years to build up, and I assembled a new one in two months. The hoodies lay forgotten in my closet.

I passed a jewelry store as I finished my food. I walked over to an overflowing trash can and wedged the container in as best I could. I looked back. *Couldn't hurt to look*, I told myself as I entered through the glass double doors.

"Is there anything I can help you with today sir?" A tall attendant with graying hair and a salt and pepper mustache had approached me. I looked at him and thought for a second. I could get something for Zoey. Or I could get something else for her.

"Sir?"

"Yes, I'd like to look at... engagement rings."

"Congratulations, sir. Right this way." He swept his arm towards a glass display at the back of the store. I started walking.

"Don't congratulate me yet. Anyone can ask. And I'm not sure I'm going to."

"Cold feet sir?" He was calm. I imagined he had had this very conversation many times before. I scanned his wrinkled fingers for a ring, but didn't find one.

"I suppose. How do you know?" He considered the question.

"I wouldn't ask me. I'm divorced, so apparently I didn't know." He walked behind the glass case. "See anything you like?"

I examined the diamonds. They all looked the same to me. I examined the price tags. The differences were vast. I pointed to a cheaper, but not the cheapest, ring towards the bottom of the display.

"I love her. But what if I wake up in a year and don't? Or if she doesn't love me?" He reached carefully between the more expensive and larger diamonds and picked out the ring I had selected. He handed it to me. I held it, unsure of what I was supposed to do with it. Surely he didn't expect me to try it on?

"If I could be frank with you, sir." He lowered his voice and looked around for his boss. "It's probably not worth the trouble. Most marriages these days end in divorce, and that can get ugly."

"Wow, what a wonderful sentiment."

"Hey, I'm just trying to save you a little money." I thought of Zoey as she kissed me, Zoey as we snuggled and watched a movie in the dark, Zoey as she pondered what to order from a place we'd been to three times already. I was angered by his doubt.

"I'll take it." I pulled out my card. "I'll buy it. Does it come with a case?" He seemed taken aback, flustered. Or perhaps he had been playing me. Either way, I had made my decision.

"Yes, yes of course." He took the ring and my card from me and found a black case. He walked over to the register. I followed him, beginning to doubt myself. Was I really buying a ring to spite some man I'd never see again in my life? But he already had my card. I didn't want to be rude. I considered the success of my mother's efforts to socially condition me. I was so afraid of offending a stranger that I would spend a thousand dollars on a ring and propose to a girl I had only met three months ago. She'd be proud, I decided, mostly of herself but maybe a little of me too.

My adversary rang me up. He swiped my card and handed it back to me.

"Would you like a bag?" I wondered if I was buying an engagement ring or a loaf of bread and a quart of milk.

"No, I'll carry it." I pocketed the ring. My khakis pressed it tight against my thigh. I was hyper aware of it. I exited the store and walked home. The sun beat down on me and I could feel my leg sweating where the ring was stuck. I took it out and held it. I wanted strangers on the street to see it, to know what I was going to do. I didn't know when I was going to ask her, if I was going to ask her. I thought about where in my apartment I could keep it. Maybe I'd ask Kevin to hold on to it for me. I imagined being married to Zoey as I walked up the stairs of my apartment.

The party "started" at 8:00. People started arriving around 9:00. Zoey had come over earlier to help me set up. This consisted of us putting out beers, chips and salsa, then fucking on the couch while *The Departed* played on the television in the background.

"Are you a cawp?" I yelled while we got dressed. She put on tight dark blue jeans and a frilly revealing green top that matched her eyes. I put on khakis and a red and yellow rugby shirt.

"I'm not a fucking cawp." She went into the kitchen and got out a bottle of wine. I'd started keeping wine in the apartment because she didn't like beer. I grabbed a beer from the cooler we had set out. It was cold. The mountains weren't blue though. We sat and watched the rest of the movie. Just as Marky-Mark made everything right and headed off into the sunset, Kevin and Murph showed up. I introduced them to Zoey. She whispered loudly to me.

"Are we sure they're not fucking cawps?" Kevin frowned. He was from Cleveland.

"Are you a cawp?" I stepped up to Murph, a fellow Bostonian. He jutted his chest out me.

"I'm not a cawp." We bumped chests. I retreated to Zoey, who was laughing. Kevin was confused, he looked at each of us.

"It's cool," I said to Zoey. "He says he's not a cawp."

"Well then I guess we should entrust him with all the tapes we made of us doing illegal things." She leaned against me. I put my arm around her.

"Sounds like a plan. You guys wanna drink? You paid for 'em." They nodded and I went off to grab beers for them. We made small talk when I came back. Zoey seemed a little nervous. More and more people arrived. Louie arrived, the girl with purple hair in tow. The two of them were the most bizarre couple. I imagined their kids having a mix of red and purple hair. Louie brought her over and introduced the group to her. I couldn't stop looking at her lips, which were painted black. She glared at me. Zoey excused herself to go to the bathroom.

"Don't talk about me too much," she called over her shoulder. We all laughed.

As soon as she was out of earshot, the reviews began. They were mostly positive.

"She's cool, man." Murph.

"I like her. I can see why you like her so much. She is gorgeous." Kevin said.

"She seems to like you a lot too." Louie said. I felt my back pocket where the ring was. I told myself not to make the same mistake I had with Amanda, to wait for a romantic moment alone.

"I don't like her." Louie's girl had spoken up. I paid attention to her voice for the first time. It was high-pitched, and had a sort of whine to it that reminded me of a hive of bees buzzing around.

"I'm sorry, who are you again?" I was irritated. "Do you even know my name?"

"Yes, you're Zach. It's your birthday." She was defiant, her black lips pouted as she eyeballed me.

"Sweetie, let's go get something to drink." Louie led her off.

"What a bitch." Zoey returned.

"Do they like me?" she asked. Kevin and Murph laughed.

"Not too much, they think you smell." I giggled.

"Very funny. What are you, about half a beer in?" She grabbed my can and took a sip. I heard the door burst open. It ricocheted off the wall and bounced back. A hand stopped it. Randy burst in. He was sweaty and out of breath. He ran over to me.

"Happy birthday buddy! Ah, and this must be the woman we've heard so much about. She does have fantastic tits, you weren't lying." He said all this very fast while shaking my hand up and down.

"Shut up," I said. "I didn't say that," I added to Zoey.

"Why? Are my tits not fantastic?" She pushed her chest up and looked down.

"Yes, they are, it's just-"

"Anyways." Randy spoke loudly. A few people looked over. He lowered his voice. "About that present I have for you." I sighed. The big reveal.

"Yes, what is it?" He put his arm around me and pulled me to him. He started to speak, then stopped. He looked around. I noticed he had pit stains on his checkered Henley. He reached into his chest pocket and removed a few tabs.

"I have managed to procure for myself, you, and, if she so desires, your lady friend a few tabs of LSD. The good stuff too. Like what Ginsberg would have used." Acid it was. I was glad it wasn't peyote. I never knew anyone even still used peyote until Brian and Randy had showed up at my door a few years ago with it. That was a weird night. Every few months they'd get some more. I didn't like it. Acid, on the other hand, was normally enjoyable. I'd only done it twice, once during freshman year with this sophomore girl I had slept with a few times, and once with Amanda and Brian a few weeks before he died. Well, not with Amanda. She had babysat, sipping on a glass of chardonnay while we deteriorated into two raving and ranting lunatics.

I looked at Zoey. We hadn't done anything harder than weed and alcohol together. She knew a little about my past with cocaine, mainly what I had told her about Brian. The 'shrooms, acid, and peyote were another story. I wondered how she would react. She grinned mischievously.

"First time for everything I guess." She took a tab from Randy and popped it in her mouth before I could say anything. I reached out a hand to grab her, but I was too slow. She looked at me. "You better have one too, I don't want to trip alone."

Randy looked at her cleavage. "You can trip with me." He raked his fingers through his greasy hair. "I'm Randy."

"Oh, give me one of those." I grabbed a tab from Randy and popped it in my mouth. The familiar bitter taste filled my mouth, stronger than I remembered it. Randy ate the last tab. I let it melt on my tongue. Zoey clutched my arm. She jumped up and down excitedly.

The party was decent at first. Everyone wanted to meet Zoey. It started to get weird after an hour or so. I felt the LSD start to take effect. I looked at Zoey, she seemed to be feeling it too. She sat on the couch staring at the ceiling. She rubbed her fingers on the pleather slowly. I went and sat next to her. She snuggled up next to me.

"Do you see that?" I looked up. The plaster ceiling had scratches on it, sure, but I didn't see anything remarkable. I rubbed my thumb and pointer finger together.

"No, what do you see?" She looked at me. She seemed to think I was lying.

"It looks like... candy bars are going to start falling from the ceiling." I giggled. She looked hurt.

"You're tripping Zoey. All these people came to meet you and we're going to sit on this couch tripping." She giggled.

"Oh no," she sat up and suddenly looked serious. "What if they don't like me?"

"Shhh, they love you. They're afraid I'm going to do something to mess it up. I'm afraid of that too." I put my arm around her and stroked her bare skin with my thumb. She shivered.

"Do you do that? I don't want you to do that." She looked like a small child when she turned to face me. I kissed her. She tasted like wildflowers on a calm spring day.

"I don't want to do that either." She kissed me back and tried to straddle me. I pushed her off. "Don't do that here, everyone is watching."

"You mean the elephants? I don't think they care." I snickered watching her face contort as she over-enunciated each word. "Is it effecting you yet? Affecting? Impacting?" I watched Randy watching the door knob. He karate-chopped it.

"I'm not sure. I'd say no, but I find my hands extremely interesting right now, and I don't normally." I held up my ten digits and showed her my paws. She kissed my palm. It tickled like a feather against the small of my back if I was hanging upside down. "And I just noticed that some of the people at this party have two heads."

"That's because they are elephants, you silly bear." She patted my head condescendingly. I nodded in understanding. They were elephants, I realized. We were all elephants.

"Do you love me?" Zoey asked. I looked at her. She had stopped smiling and was inspecting my face.

"Uh." I hesitated.

"Oh, no! You don't love me." She moved to the end of the couch and looked at me with horror.

"No! It's not that! I just think we are kind of high to be having this conversation for the first time." She pouted. "Zoey Mclemore, I love you." She smiled. She moved back to my arms. She kissed my cheek. Her tongue grazed against my skin like a cow grazing in the fields. I wanted to whip out the ring, propose, then move to a farm in New Zealand and spend the rest of my life tending cows. I pictured milking a cow. I noticed Zoey had udders where her boobs should have been. I laughed.

"I love you too, Zachary Johnston. Even if you're last name does have an extra 't'." I laughed again. "What's so funny?"

"Boobies." I looked at her udders. They were boobies again. I squeezed one with my left hand.

"Hey!" She pushed my left arm off of her. "You can't do that right now."

"Why not?" I looked around. We were in a meadow, all alone. I thought back to the party, so many hours ago, and wondered how we had gotten there. "There's no one here but flowers, and they aren't judgmental." She chuckled and leaned back, shutting her eyes.

"I hate judgmental flowers." She took my arm and put it back around me. The ring burned in my back pocket. I feared it had caught fire. Kevin sat down on the other side of me. He looked like a horse. It was Kevin, there was nothing different about his face or anything, I just realized for the first time that his spirit animal was probably a horse. Or his Patronus. I wished I wasn't a Muggle.

"Are you two all right? You're giggling awfully loudly." He looked at both of us and clomped his hooves on the ground. He put a hoof on my shoulder.

"Don't tell Kevin we are on LSD." I whispered. He shook his head.

"You realize I am Kevin, right? Zoey is on your other side." The horseman was right. I turned and looked at my girlfriend.

"You're my girlfriend." I told her simply. She nodded.

"You're my favorite cat." She patted me on the head. "Would you like some milk?"

"How strong was that shit? You guys are messed up." The horseman whinnied.

"Um, Zachy." Zoey's voice had changed. It warbled, she sounded unsure of herself.

"Yes, my darling angel?" I stared at the halo above her head. It was pink, not golden like haloes are supposed to be.

"I think I am going to bed. I need to lie down and sleep." She got up unsteadily.

"Here, let me help you." Kevin moved towards her. She shrieked. All the monkeys looked over at us. I told them everything was fine, to go back to their bananas. They kept looking.

"I'll help her." I told the horseman. He snorted out of his large black nostrils. I ran my hand through his auburn mane and wondered if I had a saddle in the apartment. We were back in the apartment, I noticed. I put Zoey's arm around my shoulders and led her off to the bedroom. It looked suspiciously yellow.

"What time is it?" She moaned. I looked at the time. The red lights twirled and danced to the slow, slow music.

"Kevin!" I yelled. He was right behind me.

"It's 11:45," He looked at the snake that was wrapped around his wrist. It hissed at me. I dropped Zoey in the bed with her feet facing the headboard. I wanted to keep her away from the porcupines at the head of the bed. Kevin grabbed one and handed it to her.

"What do I do with this purple dog?" She wondered aloud.

"It's a pillow. Just put your head on it and go to sleep." Kevin sounded exasperated. Exasperated. EXASPERATED. EEXXAAS-Sperated. I pulled on his nopple to reperate him. It didn't work. He stared at me. Laser beams shot towards me. I dropped to my knees and tried to shield myself from his low-frequency death rays. It worked. He dragged me back to the couch, which had grown eyes since I had last encountered it, many lifetimes ago. It enveloped me into its warm brown embrace. I melted into the couch. People, many of them carrying demons on their shouldery arm endings, came up to me to wish me a happy birthday. I told them that today was the day we celebrated the birth of the God-King. I noted that this was the hardest I'd ever tripped.

"Arrogant prick," one of the lions roared as he strutted away. I fired the bow and arrow I had found lying next to me at him. It missed and knocked over the bowl of chips.

"Zach! Stop throwing beer cans!" Kevin sat next to me. He restricted my arms with mind ropes.

"Where is Randall the Supplier?" I wondered. He apparated right next to me. I jumped.

"Hey man, like, shiiit." He slurred as he spoke. His mouth was filled with bananas. I wondered if he was a spy for the monkeys in the Cold War.

"You should defect." I told him.

"I do need to poop." He wandered off into the icy part of the apartment. I followed him. He closed the door in front of me. I almost waltzed into it. I caught a glimpse of igloos and penguins. I opened the door. Randy was squatting over a hole in the ice. A fishing rod came out of the hole and connected to a large Eskimo man. I threw a fish eyeball at him, but it hit Randy. He swore at me.

"Begone, you scoundrel!" Kevin came running over and pulled me out of Antarctica. I shivered as the temperature changed.

"Should I remove my upper garments?" I inquired of the dwarf who grasped my limb.

"Absolutely not." I didn't like his tone. Far too much insolence for such a minor character in the epic that was my life. All around me, chaos reigned. The entirety of the animal kingdom had wormed its way into my apartment. They all stood around talking about weather and pop culture, smartly avoiding politics or religion. *Very intelligent for farm animals*, I thought. Or I should say, neurons in my brain fired in such circuits as to convince the homunculus in my brain that I had thought such a thunky thinky thought.

"Let's go for a walk." I instructed the dwarf to fetch me my finest walking stick.

"You don't own a walking stick."

"Silly dwarf, what's this then?'

"That's a beer." I feared the shortness of the dwarf had affected his vision. I stood on the couch, taking care to avoid stepping on its eyes.

"Attention everyone, please stop grazing and address your eyeballs to my shining ghost." Laughter from around the room. Someone stopped the slow music.

"I will be exiting shortly. As this is my place of residence, I must beg you all to depart." A few groans. The rhinoceros were particularly vocal about their displeasure. "Please take as much beer as you can carry for the road. I apologize that the bacchanalia must be cut short, but I am currently, in medical terms, tripping my fucking balls off." Cheers. The hyenas howled. The crows crowed. The humans humanized the animals, assigning them human desires and facial features to better connect with them. Kevin the shepherd chased everyone out, apologizing profusely. I sang happy birthday to the couch. As it happened, he was turning two today.

"It's funny," I said, as Kevin pulled me down, "Life's little coincidences."

"Right," he said. He chugged a beer. I watched the brown liquid travel down through him into his stomach, where it set to work murdering innocent brain cells and damaging his ability to make smart decisions.

"You really shouldn't drink," I told him, waving my finger in his face. It started to fall off, but I was able to catch it in my teeth. He ignored me. "Now, let us march onwards. To July we go!" I headed out the door. I stopped and looked at him. His mouth had switched places with his nose. It wasn't a good look for him. I looked at the clock, and managed to read 11:52. "Do I need a coat?"

"It's June," he said. I wondered why he hadn't addressed the question.

"This is no time for fun facts, Franklin." I headed out the door and went to the elevator. I pushed the button, A firefly appeared inside to let me know that my button push had been successfully communicated to the elf who controlled the elevators. Kevin joined me a moment later.

"She's asleep. I think she'll sleep it off."

"This is no time for your irrelevant insinuations, Ian. Now let's see if we can speed up this elf." I banged on the doors. They opened. I stepped inside. "You're a wizard, Harry," I said to the small shy teen behind me.

"Still Kevin." He seemed tense. "Where are we going?"

"Let's let the night guide us, why don't we? And stop asking so many questions, Dumbledore will get upset." We descended on a cloud of lollipops and rainbows to the ground floor.

"I don't think I've ever seen you this messed up." Kevin held my arm in his icy grip as we exited my place of residence.

"I know," I concurred, as you always should. "'Howl' might even make sense to me right now."

We made our way down the barren landscape, the desolate criss-crossing of buildings and shops and stands and life. I noticed a sign for 9th street, and the nine came too close for comfort. Everything was intense. Colors were way more vibrant. It was life, just more-so than normal. Kevin walked closely behind me. I skipped down (or geographically up, I suppose) fourth avenue. We traveled for hours without saying a word. I saw a rat scurry down the street in the opposite direction.

I grew wearied from the traveling. We passed a sign for 10ᵗʰ street, and I laughed at the number of digits ten required to express the same info as nine. I realized nine had more letters than ten, and grew quiet. When I realized eight had even more, I began to suspect a conspiracy. I turned to tell Kevin about the government ruining this once great nation, but noticed Batman was hanging around on the other side of the street. I ran across to him. Horns blared and brakes screeched, some asshole had almost caused a car accident.

"There is crime nearby." I spoke in a gravelly voice. Batman looked at me, curiously. "I have reason to suspect illegal drugs have been ingested by that man. I pointed at the window of the store he was standing next to.

"Are you pointing to your reflection?" His voice was disappointingly normal. And his fangs were smaller than I had expected.

"Who else but the Mirror people would you expect to commit such atrocities? We must burn our clothes if we are to scare them off." I took off my shirt. Kevin had finally managed to cross the street. He tried to grab me, but I was wearing ice skates and easily skated around him. Batman watched me. He pulled handcuffs from his utility belt. They squirmed in his hands.

I removed my pants. Batman grabbed me. I tried to skate away, but he put the worm-cuffs on my hands. "Sir, you are under arrest. What did he take?" He addressed Kevin.

"You'll never take me alive! Kevin, don't let him make you an envelope!" I squirmed. My eyes felt heavy. Kevin patted me on the shoulder and whispered to Batman. I noticed for the first time that he was dressed in a red shirt with green short sleeves and a yellow cape. His thighs were much more toned than the last time I had seen them.

"What gym do you go to? Do you even lift, bro?" My vision, which had been blurry for some time, began to swirl. Somewhere in the dark recesses of my brain, the sober part of me cried out, quietly reminding me that I was likely just hitting the peak of what would be at least an 8 hour trip. I descended down the rabbit hole, farther into myself than I had ever gone...

Chapter 10

I sit at a desk. A man in a suit hands me some forms across the desk. He is an accountant. I look around the office. Everything is grey. I try to read the print on the degrees behind his desk but cannot. I fill out the tax forms. I am home. I sit at my desk, laptop open in front of me. I return some phone calls, send a few emails. I put some old photos together into an album. I upload it to Facebook. It gets a few likes. I make tea. I watch tennis on TV. One player wins easily over the other. I cannot pronounce either of their names.

I am in the bathroom, I brush my teeth. I shave. I shower. I look in the mirror and I am a square man. There are no curves to my face. Everything is a perfect right angle. I go to work and see nobody there. I do all my work quickly. I go to Bob's old desk. I do all his work. I write line after line of perfect code. I do not make a single mistake as I write game after game. I see no one in all the time I am there.

I am home again. I go to bed. The sheets are perfectly tucked in. I slide under it and lie perfectly straight, looking up at the ceiling tiles. They are all white, perfectly smooth. There is not a flaw in the entire room. I close my eyes slowly.

* * *

I woke up in a hospital bed. Kevin was sitting by my side. He looked ragged, as if he had stayed up all night. He had. He scratched his stubbly chin and looked at me when I woke up.

"Welcome back to reality." He put his hand on my arm. My hand had one of those thingies on it that measures your pulse through your pointer finger. I watched the green line bounce on the monitor.

"What happened?" I looked around. Nurses and doctors rushed around from one patient to the next.

"You were arrested for public intoxication, public nudity, and resisting arrest. Though you didn't really resist so much as pass out." He laughed. I didn't see what was so funny.

"Where's Zoey?"

"She's at home. She woke up and went home. She was surprisingly fine. She'll probably be here in a bit. They're going to keep you here while you rehydrate." he answered my next question before I had the chance to ask it. I shifted in my bed and felt the scratchy hospital gown. I went to itch my arm and found the IV. I watched the clear fluid go into my arm for a few moments. Kevin waited for me to speak.

"Am I in trouble?" I sounded like a little kid talking to his kindergarten teacher.

"I posted bail, you should probably get a lawyer. Your friend 'Batman' said he thinks you'll probably be able to plea to a fine considering you didn't hurt anyone. He also advises you lay off the LSD for a while."

"As do I." A doctor in blue scrubs with a weary expression had made his way over to my bed. His face was at least three-quarters beard. His white hair poked out from under a blue cap he was wearing. "I haven't seen that much in somebody since the 60's." He was holding a file.

"Is Randy okay?" I remembered finally that there had been three of us who had taken the drug. My mind was foggy, all I wanted was to go home and sleep for days.

"He's fine. Apparently he has a much higher tolerance than you two." Kevin smiled to himself. "He's probably been building up to taking that much."

"Right. Well, I would advise you, and all your friends, to not take hallucinogenic drugs. Particularly in your current state. From what Mr. Bateman here tells me, you had a pretty bad trip. Adding more to your current state could permanently unsettle you." He looked at me down the bridge of his long nose. I nodded.

"I won't, I don't normally anyways, it's just-"

"I don't need an explanation, just don't do it again." He smiled at me. "I was young once, Mr. Johnston, and I was young during the sixties. I understand. Just not again." I nodded and said nothing.

When I got home from the hospital a few hours later, I spent ten or fifteen minutes on Facebook looking for any friends who had gone to law school. None of them had. I sighed and picked up my phone. I called Amanda. She was surprised to hear from me, but agreed to help me with my case. She said she would talk to one of the partners at her office and get back to me.

I felt bad just calling her for help, so I asked how she was. She sounded pleasantly surprised. We talked for almost half an hour. I started to remember why we had been best friends before we dated. We made plans to meet up, get coffee and catch up. I promised to introduce her to Zoey, she promised not to hate her too much.

* * *

A few days later, Zoey and I were lying in bed. I was checking email, and Zoey was reading a novel. She had just started *Cat's Cradle* at my recommendation. "It's my favorite book," I had told her.

"Well then I guess I'd better pretend to like it no matter what, huh?" she had shot back.

We had been doing more and more of that, just being together without talking or interacting. It was peaceful, to be able to spend so much time together without feeling the need to talk. I enjoyed being alone, but I enjoyed being alone with Zoey even more. I had always considered myself a solitary person, but I was starting to understand that I could be a solitary person while being with someone else. It was great, it really was, to be able to-

"So are we just not going to talk about it?" Zoey's words snapped me out of my reverie. I looked over. She was eyeing me over the thick rims of her reading glasses. She looked like a stern librarian. Then she turned towards me, and the comforter slipped off, revealing her revealing choice of lingerie. A sexy stern librarian.

"Bout what?" I racked my brain for what she wanted to discuss. Surely not the acid trip? I had always tried to avoid discussing anything that happened while on hallucinogens. I needed to know that I could say anything I wanted while on them without fear of repercussion, else I'd feel restrained and not enjoy the trip.

"Do you love me?" She searched my face for the answer. But the question was different. Before, it had been needy, desperate almost. Now, it was practical, but not cold. Just... guarded.

"I meant everything I said, Zoey." I smiled at her, and slid my computer off my lap. I took her hand in mine and leaned forward. "I love you."

She smiled wide. Her eyebrows relaxed. Some weight lifted off of her. I hadn't noticed, but she had tensed up when she asked. "I love you too, Zachary." She spoke quickly and kissed me hard. "I was afraid you had only said it because of the drugs."

I laughed. "Well, that certainly made it easier to say. But it is true. And to be honest, that scares me." I slid the blanket off of me and eased myself out of bed.

"Well. I didn't realize I was scary." She pretended to be offended. "Where are you going?" I stretched my arms out. I was wearing nothing but boxers. Zoey watched my abs move as I stretched.

"I'm going to grab some water before bed, you want anything?" She got up and put her glasses on the bed.

"I'll come with you, assuming that doesn't frighten you." Apparently we weren't done with this topic.

"You know what I mean. I've never..." I trailed off. I wasn't sure if I wanted to admit it.

"What? Said it before?" Her tone was one of curiosity, not disbelief. I walked into the kitchen.

"No, yeah, I mean, I've said it before. Just not regularly. I mean, I haven't been in a long term relationship where we both say-"

"Zach, relax. This doesn't have to change anything." She had followed me into the kitchen. She hugged me from behind as I grabbed a glass from the cabinet above the sink. I was tense.

"I know, I just, I mean, what now? I never said it to Amanda till the end, because I didn't want to marry her." I stopped short of finishing the thought. I thought of the ring, tucked safely in the back pocket of the cargo shorts I had worn that day, which were lying... where? I scanned the kitchen.

"Now? I don't know. Nothing has to change. I mean, I've only had one relationship before where I said it. And that ended... poorly." I filled the glass with tap water. Zoey released me and crossed her arms. I sipped from the glass as I walked back to bed, Zoey close behind. I still hadn't really looked her in the eye since I had said it.

"Was that with...Ryan?" I looked over my shoulder at her as I got into bed. She flinched almost imperceptibly. I knew no one would have seen it except for me. I liked that. Not the flinch itself, but the intimacy that allowed me to see it.

"Yes." She seemed closed off. We had never really discussed our exes. She knew I had broken up with Amanda shortly before meeting her, but not much else. The only thing I knew about Ryan was that they had dated for almost four years.

"What happened? We don't have to talk about it. But you can tell me, if you want." I wanted to seem comforting without being nosy. It was a difficult line to tiptoe. Zoey weighed my words.

"He cheated on me." She slid back under the comforter. I put the glass of water on the bedside table, next to my charging phone and too-thin wallet. I waited.

"It... I..." she stopped. I moved closer to her. She scooched over to me and wrapped her arms around me. I rested my head on her head and stroked her upper arm. She spoke into my chest.

"It wasn't just once. The first time, we hadn't said it yet. He said it would never happen again. He took me out that night and told me he loved me. I didn't say it to him for several months after that. Finally, I trusted him again. I told him I loved him." She sniffled, and I tried to see if she was going to cry. "The second time, which wasn't actually the second time, I caught him. With one of my friends. We weren't close, but she told me later that they had been sleeping together for months.

Felt terrible about it, she said. I wish I had said something. But I just cried. I couldn't look at her."

"That sucks," I said. I was cautious. Saying the wrong thing could start a fight.

"Yes, it does." Her tone was bitter. "We had a long drawn out fight, aired all the dirty laundry any couple has after four years. He blamed me."

"What a dick." Zoey barely even seemed to hear me.

"For a long time, I thought he made some valid points. I blamed myself for not being there for him." She looked up at me, tears welling up in her green eyes. I had never seen her cry before. "Isn't that ridiculous? I was so weak. It took me a long time to get over him." I stroked her hair.

"You were young, it's not your fault how you felt…" The pictures of Zoey and Ryan, that I had seen months ago when I Facebook-stalked her, came rushing back to me. How happy she had seemed. And it had all gone horribly wrong. Could that happen to us? I noticed my shorts with the ring in them by the door. Was there a bulge in the pocket? Or was I just imagining things?

"It took me a long time to realize what a scumbag he was. And even longer to consider dating again. You are the first person I've trusted since him." She said this slowly, watching me as she enunciated each word. And there it was. She was absolutely, completely vulnerable. She had given herself to me entirely. I vowed to never hurt her. Her vulnerability mirrored the feelings I had been developing for weeks, the scary yet tantalizing discovery that I wanted, no, I needed to tell her everything about me and wanted to know everything about her. I thought of Amanda, we were getting coffee soon, catching up.

"I have to tell you something, it's not a big deal." I searched her eyes for answers, for the best phrasing.

"What?" she seemed fearful.

"I will never hurt you." She relaxed, smiling a sad smile.

"Yes, you will. We all hurt the people we love, no matter how hard we try not to." I kissed her forcefully.

"I'm meeting with Amanda soon." I broke off the kiss and tried to power through my explanation as quickly as possible. "I needed a lawyer after, you know, and she works in a legal office and she set me up with a partner at her firm, and we got to talking, and I think it would be healthy if we caught up a little, we were very good friends, and it means nothing, and I don't want you to worry-"

"It's okay, Zach, I get it." She was trying to convince herself. "Thank you for telling me. It means a lot that you would do that."

"Whew. Good, I didn't want that to be an issue. I love you." It was out there, we could say it whenever we wanted. It wasn't scary, it was freeing.

"I love you. Now, let's change to a happier subject." She kissed me and pulled me onto her.

"Okay," I laughed and kissed her forehead. She whispered to me. "Do we have any condoms?"

"Yeah, let me…" I leaned over to the bedside table.

"Wait…" Zoey grabbed me as I turned away. "I'm actually, well, I'm on the pill."

"You are?" I remembered a similar conversation with Amanda, after a few weeks of dating. I knew where she was going. I kissed Zoey fiercely. She didn't need to spell it out. We understood each other.

* * *

Amanda and I met a few weeks later at the Starbucks on West 4th. It was much less crowded now that NYU's semester was over. I got there first and got my usual black coffee. Miranda wasn't there. I was served by a tall black guy with long dreads and bad acne. I took a table in the corner, away from the wannabe writers and summer students typing away on their MacBooks. I watched the people pass by outside. A mother led her two young sons across the street to the park. They fought behind her, each trying to tear a plastic dinosaur away from the other. The sun was in my eyes, but I think it was a t-rex. The bell jingled, and I turned to the door. Amanda walked in. She looked like she had gained some muscle since I last saw her. She was wearing a grey pantsuit, and had her hair up in a bun. She smiled when she saw me. There was no line, and she quickly got her tea and a muffin and came over to join me.

"I don't have much time, I gotta get back to work soon." She spoke as she walked over to the table. I stood up and hugged her. She wrapped her arms around me and I smelled her muffin. My stomach growled. I considered getting one for myself. She sat down across from me.

"That's fine. How are you?" I genuinely wanted her to be happy. I had no ill will towards her whatsoever.

"I'm doing okay, how are you? How are things working out with Jerry?" Jerry was the partner she had helped me hire from her office at a discounted rate.

"It's good. He thinks we'll be able to plea down to just a fine. So, not too bad." I took a sip of my coffee. It was still too hot.

"Most expensive acid you ever had, I'd bet." She took the wrapper off her muffin and bit into it. I laughed.

"Yeah, probably." I took the cover off my coffee. Steam rose from it. She looked me over.

"How's Zoey?" she asked, finally. I smiled. Any mention of her name brought a smile to my face.

"She's great. Everything is just so... so right. I don't want to compare, but you know what our relationship was like those last few months. We had to work so hard. With Zoey, everything just fits." I stopped talking. A flicker of a frown had crossed her face when I mentioned our time together. She seemed darker now, somehow. I regretted hurting her.

"That's, that's wonderful Zach. I'm happy for you." She took a sip of her tea. I looked out the window.

"Listen, Amanda, I don't know about you, but I think I'm ready to be friends again." I turned to her. "We were great friends before we dated. I like you a lot. I'd like you to be a part of my life." She didn't react.

"Zaaach..." She seemed reluctant to respond. I put the cover back on my coffee. "I think I'm still getting over the way we parted. Seeing you, it-"

"The best way to get over however you feel is to hang out with your old friends again. Come out some night with us, like you used to, before everything. It'll be like we're at NYU again." She stood up. She grabbed what was left of her muffin and her tea.

"I should go, I need to get back to work." She turned to leave.

"Amanda." She stopped but didn't face me. "Just come out and spend one night with us, please. For the others, not even for me." She looked at me. Her face seemed so much older than I remembered it.

"Fine. I really do have to go now." She left. I sat there, people-watching while I sipped my coffee until it was cold enough to drain in one gulp. As I left, I tossed my cup in the overflowing trash can. It bounced out. I wanted to keep walking, and I did for a few feet. But then I turned and went back. I carried the cup for a few blocks until I found a can that was only half full. I tossed the cup away.

She met up with us a few weeks later at Brad's. It was depressingly hot. A record day, they said. Everyone cheered when she sat down at our table. She blushed. She was wearing a summer dress and flats. She looked radiant. Zoey couldn't make it, she had a lot of work at her new job. She told me she'd try to come over later. I knew that meant she almost certainly wouldn't. Kevin and Randy ended up sitting next to her. I looked around the bar. I had been through a lot in the six years I had been coming here. I saw, for the first time, a time in the near future when I would no longer come here. I felt the ring in my back pocket. I had taken to carrying it around. I was afraid to leave it in my apartment. When Zoey got the munchies, she turned the whole place over, even the bathroom and the living room, looking for chips or jerky or other things to occupy her mouth. So I brought the ring around with me. I hadn't showed it to anyone, hadn't even hinted about it to Zoey. We had started saying "I love you" after my birthday party. I had never reached that place with a girl before. I told the group there that. Amanda got quiet. She was the first girl I had ever said that to and meant it, and we had broken up minutes later. I wondered if we'd ever be able to get back to where we had been before. Probably not.

I got up and went to the bar without saying anything. There were two blond girls sitting at the bar. They turned and watched me expectantly. They wore torn-up tank tops and very short jean shorts. It was summer, after all. Their legs were tan and long. I wondered how Kevin and the guys would decide which one they liked better. They looked identical to me, though I knew they weren't. I walked up to them. The girl on the right smiled, flashing her blue eyes and long lashes at me.

"Excuse me," I said. I was in between both of them.

"Yes?" Blue eyes looked me up and down. I was wearing khaki shorts and a Pete Maravich jersey that Kevin had loaned me. We had gone to West 4th earlier to play some ball. I ended up just watching after my back started hurting. I had taken one shot and felt it. So I hadn't bothered to change. Besides, who did I need to impress? Zoey wasn't coming, and she had told me anyways that she didn't care what I wore, she just wanted it off as soon as possible. So the jersey would be fine with her, if I ever saw her.

"I'm just trying to get to the bar." I asked the bartender for a pitcher of Dos Equis, the cheapest beer they had on tap. All about efficiency.

"Oh." Blue eyes noticed my Adidas flip flops. "Nice sandals." She laughed.

"Look, just because I'm not going to hit on you doesn't mean you get to trash my outfit." I paid for the pitcher and left before she could respond. I heard her whispering angrily to her friend. I was so sick of the bar scene. I was a full fledged stage two man. The ring moved as I sat down. I put down the pitcher and five cups. Kevin and Randy and Murph poured themselves beer. Louie was off with that goth chick, I still couldn't remember her name.

Amanda got a beer next. I took what was left of the pitcher and filled myself a cup. With the little remaining, I topped everyone off. Everyone made the requisite good hearted comments about what a great man I was for buying the first pitcher. I checked my phone. Nothing from Zoey.

Time passed, drinks flowed, inhibitions dropped. We reminisced. Amanda, who had been so cold to me at the beginning of the night, was laughing at my ridiculous puns and corny anecdotes by the time we were a few pitchers in. We watched our single male friends hit on girls with little success. Randy left with a Puerto Rican girl who was wearing less clothing than I'd ever seen a girl wear in a bar. Her jean shorts barely covered her ass, and her shirt was nothing more than a bra with a little extra coverage of her cleavage. Randy made a face at me as he left. *Can you believe how lucky I am?* He asked non-verbally. His Juliet almost fell over. He carried her out the door. "Don't rape her," I wanted to call after him.

"I can't believe I used to hit on girls here." Kevin and Amanda were sitting with me still, each sipping on a gin and tonic, courtesy of me. I had finished my last beer ten minutes or so earlier. Kevin got angry.

"Oh, you're so much better than us, now that you're with Zoooey, is that it?" He burped. Amanda and I looked at him.

"I think you've had too much, Kev." I patted him on the back.

"I'm fine I…Just want to take a nap." He put his head down on the table.

"Okay, bedtime. C'mon buddy, let's go." I got up and pulled him up by his armpits. He groaned. "I'm gonna take him home", I said to Amanda. "Where's Murph?" She pointed to the bar. He was making out with Blue Eyes.

"I'll come with you." Amanda finished her drink quickly. I finished Kevin's. He moaned and swung his hands at me. I put one of his arms around me and Amanda took the other. We carried him out of the bar.

"I love you guys." Kevin slurred as we stepped out into the humid July heat.

"We know." I hailed a cab. "I'm not going to carry him all the way back to midtown." Kevin perked up when I opened the door.

"I'm good," he said. Standing straight up, he walked easily over to the cab and got in. "You guys don't have to come all the way up to midtown with me. I'll be fine."

Amanda and I shared a look. "Are you sure?" she asked. "It's not a big deal." Kevin shut the door and put his head out the window.

"I'll be fine. Why is it so fucking hot?"

"Milk was a bad choice." I told him. Amanda laughed. The cab pulled away. I stepped onto the curb, a little wobbly.

"Steady, sailor," Amanda grinned as she placed her hand on the small of my back.

"Shiiiit," I said. "I'm drunk too."

"You wanna go back inside?" She looked at Brad's with disdain.

"No. I think I might be over Brad's. I'm gonna go home and watch a movie or something while hoping Zoey comes over." I started walking. Amanda didn't move.

"Are you going home?" I said. Our eyes locked.

"I guess so. I'm that way too." She started walking too.

We walked in silence for a few blocks. One of us said something, I don't remember what, that broke the tension. We were both pretty drunk. I sang Outkast and she pointed out that I was still tone-deaf.

"Zoey didn't fix your sense of pitch," she said, somewhat bitterly. We had arrived at my apartment. "I'm so not tired. I feel like the night has just begun."

"Yeah," I said, not really listening. I checked my phone again. Still nothing from Zoey. It was almost 1:00. "You wanna watch a movie or something?" The question hung in the air. We looked at each other. Sober Zach tried to protest, but he was shouted down.

"Sure."

We went up to my apartment and argued over what to watch. We ended up flipping through the channels until we found *Dodgeball* was on. There was no debate, we had watched this movie together so many times before we just had to watch it again. I put the remote down and went to grab us some beers. We had both been sitting on the couch. When I returned, I took the recliner. We silently watched commercials. The movie came back on.

"You got another one of these?" Amanda had finished her beer. I didn't respond, my phone vibrated at the same time. *Almost done, can come over in 30 or so. Should i? Sure*, I texted back. I got up and took the empty from Amanda. I finished mine as well and threw both in the recycling bin by the fridge. I grabbed two more and popped mine open. I sat down on the couch just as Ben Stiller offered Vince Vaughn 50,000 dollars to throw the final match. I handed the beer to Amanda. She pulled the tab.

"Cheers." She tapped her beer against mine. Our hands touched. Her skin was cold and clammy. The room was unbearably hot. My brain soaked in a warm alcohol bath, and I knew if I shut my eyes I'd be asleep instantly.

"I think having the windows open is somehow making it hotter in here," I said. I considered getting up to shut them, but I was too lazy and only half-serious.

"I always told you to get an air conditioner." She smirked at me. The movie went to commercials. I glanced in her direction. We were closer than we should have been. I scooched away.

"You always told me a lot of things." I didn't say it in a mean way, but I was afraid she took it that way. She frowned. My words were not matching my thoughts.

"I was kind of bossy." She laughed, and I joined in. The movie came back on. My balls were ridiculously sweaty. I scratched them, trying to move them to a more comfortable position. Amanda fidgeted uncomfortably.

The underdogs won, as they always did. We had somehow gotten closer to each other as we each finished yet another beer. Peter Lafleur enjoyed his victory kiss. We looked at each other…

And the door burst open. Zoey came in. "I am so exhausted. Let's just go to be-" She stopped talking. Amanda and I were not touching. We were sitting close to each other, but not that close. The sounds from the television covered an awkward pause. I opened my mouth to speak but no words arrived. Amanda popped up.

"You must be Zoey. So great to finally meet you. I'm Amanda." She approached, hand outstretched. Zoey shook it slowly.

"Amanda, as in ex-girlfriend Amanda?" She was looking right at me. I nodded once.

"Yes." Amanda stood there smiling.

"Why are you hanging out and drinking alone with your ex-girlfriend at two in the morning on a Friday night?" I resented the question. I loved Zoey and would never cheat on her. That's not what I said.

"Because my current girlfriend works all the time and I never see her." In my head it sounded like a joke, but even drunk off my ass when I heard it I knew it was bad. "I'm sorry, I didn't mean that... We were just watching television-"

Amanda cut me off. "It was nothing like that, we were all hanging out at the bar and-"

"You know I love you and would never do anything like what you're implying-"

"Just stop!" Zoey seethed. It occurred to me that she was the only one sober. "I don't want to hear it. Yes, I work all the time. I didn't realize you couldn't go a night without female companionship of some kind."

"That's not fair, she was one of my best friends long before I ever met you, and-"

"How dare you." She said it quietly, but the look of fury on her face shut me up. "I'll be leaving now. Don't call me." She turned her back to me; her shoulders were taut and tensed like a bowstring ready to fire.

"Zoey, c'mon I'm drunk, I didn't mean it like that-" I walked towards her and tripped over a lacrosse stick that was lying on the floor. I stumbled, but regained my balance.

"I don't care how you meant it. Enjoy her. He likes it when you pinch his nipples," she added to Amanda. Amanda looked like she was going to cry. Zoey surprisingly did not. She just looked like she wanted to murder someone. I felt horrible and wanted to vomit. I realized with a start that I had tears in my eyes.

"No!" I screamed. The weight of my intoxication enveloped me, yet failed to cover the swelling of fear and shame in the pit of my belly. "I don't! Zoey, stop."

Zoey hesitated, glanced at Amanda, then back to me.

"You don't what?" She said, her legs still pointed towards the door.

Time slowed, I felt my legs churning as I approached her. I wanted to hug her, to hold her close so she knew she was it for me. My legs could gain no traction, and the silence stretched onwards. Before I knew what was happening I was filling it with words.

"I don't like it when she pinches my nipples I like it when you do! I don't want you to stop- fuck, no, that's not… I want- You, I, always… fuck! Zoey, my words, words, words… are not working."

"Well put." Zoey's sarcasm cut through me. I kept going, hoping to power through the drunken mess to some sober mea culpa, the magic phrase that would put all this tension back in the box and close it up real shut.

"I love you, Zoey."

"Good for you, Zach." She left.

"I love her," I said. Amanda walked over to me and put her hand on my shoulder.

"I know." The fear and shame converted to rage. I shook Amanda's hand off me.

"I love *her*, okay?" I glared at Amanda, my ex, Amanda, my friend, Amanda, my enemy. She winced. I grabbed her half full beer off the coffee table.

"Jesus Christ, Zach. You think I don't know that?"

Anger coursed through my veins like heroin, filling every part of me with an urge to erase the past hour, the whole night, Amanda.

"THEN WHAT ARE YOU DOING HERE?" I roared. I gesticulated with the beer and Amanda flinched like I might throw it. Her eyes were wide but unlike Zoey she wasn't angry. She was afraid.

"I'm sorry," I whispered. Amanda hung her head. I wasn't mad at her, I was mad at me.

"I should go."

"She thinks we…." I couldn't finish the thought. Amanda went over to the door.

"It shouldn't be hard to convince her you don't want me…" she muttered.

"I don't want to hurt her." I barely heard what Amanda said.

"…I believe you," she called, and slammed the door. I chugged the rest of her beer as I entered my bedroom. I crushed the empty can and threw it at the window. The exertion threw me off balance and I tumbled onto my bed headfirst. I needed my phone, where was my phone? I felt something in my back pocket and pulled it out. I tossed the ring box on my nightstand and it opened. The diamond ring stared at me.

"Yuck Fou," I slurred, my eyelids drooping as the room began to spin. Darkness overcame me.

Chapter 11

I awoke gently for once-what time was it? I grabbed my phone off my nightstand and rubbed my eyes. Shit. It was still only 8:00. There was no way I could talk to Zoey yet. I tried to go back to sleep. I was too nervous. I felt a pit in my stomach as I imagined life without Zoey. I had been the happiest I had ever been these past few months, and I was terrified that a misunderstanding would end a relationship that I wanted to last forever. I glanced at the little black box on my night table. It taunted me.

I lay in bed for over an hour before dragging myself out of bed. I was tired, but restless. I brushed my teeth and showered. I shaved carefully, making sure not to cut myself and mess up my face. Everything seemed dulled, grey. I considered having a beer, but decided it was too early. Alcohol had got me into this mess, I wasn't going to use it to ignore it. I got dressed, then decided to wear something else. I spent an hour changing outfits and posing in front of my mirror, trying to decide which would do enough to show I cared and remind her of the good times we had together. I rehearsed a speech in front of the mirror in each outfit. I finally settled on a checkered button-down, unbuttoned over a Beatles t-shirt. I paired it with some corduroy pants that she had bought me a few weeks ago. I'd be hot, but I didn't care. I looked out the window, it looked like it was going to rain. The gloomy skies threatened to ruin everyone's day. I checked the weather on my phone just to be sure. It agreed.

I sat in front of the television for an hour or so, but I wasn't really watching. I fidgeted, waiting for a time when it would be okay to call Zoey. I knew she wouldn't answer, but I wanted to try before I went over to her place. I pictured her, sitting at home on her plump overstuffed couch, in her short shorts and men's t-shirt, calling all her friends, gabbing away about me. They had never liked me, I was sure of it. I hated the fact that she had so many male friends that she knew from school. I imagined them comforting her, explaining that physicists and programmers just shouldn't mix. I seethed. I squeezed the couch. It was 11:30. Late enough. I called Zoey. I lay back on the couch. It rang and rang. I tapped the phone against my head in time with the tone.

"Hi, this is Zoey, I can't come to the phone right now, but-" I hung up, angrily jabbing the end button with my thumb. I sighed. I was exhausted, and hungover. My muscles ached. I pulled myself off the couch and went into the kitchen. I opened the fridge, there was no food except for some roast beef. I sniffed it. It was spoiled. I chucked it in the garbage. I made a mental note to take the trash out before it stunk up the place. I wished for a joint. I went into the bedroom and looked in my closet. I found a baggie with a little weed. I looked for the vaporizer, then reconsidered. I didn't want to be high when I went to Zoey's. The desire to smoke left me. For the first time in a long time, I wanted nothing more than to be sober, to make up for my mistakes. I grabbed an umbrella and headed out the door.

My stomach rumbled as I walked up Broadway to Zoey's apartment. I hoped her roommates weren't there. The less people she had tell her I was an asshole, the better. I cursed myself for talking to her the way I had. I didn't know what had gotten into me. Sure, it upset me that I didn't get to see her that much, but I understood. She was in a new job, doing research for some company into weaponizing something or other, it all flew over my head whenever she attempted to explain it to me.

Neither of us really understood the work the other one was doing. She was terrible with computers, and I had never been able to visualize ideas like that cat being dead and alive at the same time. I thought it helped us. We didn't talk about our work, we talked about the other stuff we liked. And when we wanted to vent about what was bothering us at work, the other person would just agree with every point they made because they had no idea what we were talking about. I passed a dollar pizza place and decided to eat a slice on the way over. I stepped inside, there was no door. I went over to the register and rested my arms on the green countertop. I leaned forward, putting half my weight on my arms. A short dark-skinned man with wrinkled eyes and a weary grimace asked me what I wanted.

"Slice of cheese, please." I handed over a grubby one dollar bill. He grabbed it and slid a piece of pizza out of the rotating display. He handed it on a paper plate to me along with a few napkins. I stuffed the umbrella into my back pocket. I hadn't brought the ring. I thanked him and set off up Broadway, cautiously holding the plate as close to my mouth as I could. I didn't want to talk to Zoey with cheese all over my face. I was as nervous for this conversation as I had been before our second first date. More, really. Back then she had just been an idea, a fictionalization of what I thought she might be, someone I might like. Now she was the woman I wanted to marry, to have kids with. And I would lose her if I didn't say the right things. I picked up a cup of coffee and a croissant from Starbucks. I held the cup and brown paper bag in my left hand and shifted the plate and pizza to my right. I put the slice, which was about half gone, in my mouth and held it.

I threw out the plate, still covered in melted cheese, as I arrived at Zoey's apartment. I stood outside and finished the slice. I knew the door would be locked. An old lady with a dog walked up and unlocked the door. I grabbed the door just as it was about to close. The poodle barked at me. It had a little pink bow around its neck instead of a collar. The lady eyed me suspiciously. I gave her my best non-threatening White Guy smile and waited for her to keep walking. She turned around and led her dog up the stairs. I pretended to have to tie my shoe so that I didn't have to walk right behind her. I took the stairs slowly, one at a time.

When I got to the fifth floor, I walked over to Zoey's door and raised my hand to knock. I hesitated. I turned to go, I was too nervous. My heart was beating; my palms were sweaty. I knocked gently with the backs of my fingers. I leaned against the door frame and looked out down the stairs. I held the coffee in one hand and the bag with the croissant in the other. There was no answer. After a minute or two, I knocked louder, banging on the door with my hand balled into a fist. Still no answer. I slid down the wall until my butt hit the floor. I stretched out my legs. I took out the umbrella and threw it off to my side. I could wait. I closed my eyes to clear my thoughts.

"Zach? What are you doing here?" I awoke with a start. I had slumped over. I was still holding the coffee and bag. The coffee was cold. I looked up. Zoey was at the head of the stairs holding a shopping bag from Lord and Taylor's and an umbrella. I shook my head, groggy from my unplanned catnap.

"I came to apologize." I stood up. She walked over to the door and unlocked it, shifting the umbrella underneath her arm to do so. It wasn't wet. She waited for me to continue talking. "Uh, I brought you this." I offered her the bag and cold coffee as I followed her into her apartment. The yellow walls were too happy. I looked at the poster of Ringo Starr she had over the overstuffed couch. He smiled at me. "Sorry if it's cold," I added.

She took the coffee and the bag. She went over to the kitchen and put her foot on the pedal to open the trash can. She threw out the coffee and looked in the bag. She put the bag on the wooden center island. Her kitchen was cluttered, but clean. Everything was painted in light colors. Her refrigerator was a light green, almost blue, with magnet-letters on it. I thought the Z, C, and H were all aligned, but I wasn't sure. A picture of her and her mother was pinned on the freezer door, which was right above the fridge door. A white landline was set up on the counter next to the fridge, with a legal notepad next to it. The top sheet had been torn in half. The scrap was crumpled and on the top of the recycling bin by the island, right next to Zoey's boot-covered feet. She took off her boots. Her toenails were painted black. I looked at her feet against the backdrop of the large beige tiles.

"Thank you." She looked at me. She didn't seem too upset. We stood there, her behind the center island and me in the doorway, looking at each other. Yesterday we would have been all over each other, but today there was a tension holding both of us back. Or holding her back, really.

"Look, Zoey, I'm sorry. I never should have said what I said. I love how hard you work, I think it's amazing. I was just upset that I don't ever get to see you. I love you, and I love every minute I spend with you." I said all this in a rush, eager to get past the tension. Why couldn't we just pretend it had never happened? I walked towards her. She started to embrace me.

"Good." She leaned in. I leaned in. She stopped. "And?"

"And?" I echoed. She crossed her arms.

"Are you done apologizing?"

"What else did I do?" she stiffened. I backed away. I picked up an orange and tossed it from one hand to the other.

"I found you, alone with your ex-girlfriend, getting drunk and watching a movie at 2:00 in the morning."

"Yeah, but nothing happened." I was confused. I knew she was coming over last night, didn't she realize that?

"It's not what happened, Zach, it's that you would think that's okay without telling me." She frowned at me.

"Zoey, I knew you were coming over last night, remember? We were waiting for you. I wanted you to meet Amanda." I approached her, putting the orange on the island.

"I couldn't meet her some other time?" her voice got higher. "Zach, you proposed to this girl a week before we met, you can't really expect me to be okay with you two hanging out." She picked up the orange and walked around me, her head pointed down and away from me.

"Oh, so you're forbidding me to hang out with her? She's one of my best friends." A rush of anger flowed through me, replacing the nervous energy from before.

"I'm not forbidding you to do anything. I'm asking you to be a rational adult and tell me when you're planning on having alone time with the last woman you slept with before me." I had no plans to tell her the last woman I had slept with was a girl who I imagined was currently trying desperately to buy a fake id. I didn't think it would reflect too well on me. I noticed she no longer had her television.

A puffy red winter coat was lying on the glass table where the set had rested. Odd.

"I thought you trusted me." I raised my voice. Did she really think I would cheat?

"I thought I did too. And I trusted my ex, and look where that got me." I thought back to what she had told me, about how I was the first person she had trusted since him.

"Zoey, I would never cheat on you. I love you, why isn't that enough for you?" I softened my tone and stepped towards her.

"I love you too, Zach, but I don't know if I trust you. And I can't be with someone I don't trust." She started to cry. She crossed her arms. I wanted to hold her, to comfort her. But I was the problem.

"What are you saying? You don't want to be with me?" My voice wavered. I couldn't believe where this was going. "Because of Amanda? Please don't do this."

"I'm not saying that, okay? I just need some time to think." Fuck it. I lost. Fine.

"You take all the time you need." I snapped at her. I walked out. I heard her scream as the door shut. I felt like yelling as well.

I walked around, aimlessly wandering. I didn't get what I had done to lose her trust. Amanda could be waiting for me, naked on my bed and begging for me when I came home, and the first thing I'd do was cover my eyes and tell her to leave. I was done fucking around, I was solidly in stage two, even if Randy no longer remembered what that meant. I texted Kevin and asked him to meet me that night at Brad's. I needed to talk. I thought of Brian. I was ashamed at how infrequently he crossed my mind these days. I tried to picture him. His face was hazy. I went to his Facebook page on my phone. I stared at his handsome profile picture and wanted to cry. He would have known what to do. Kevin's advice would be a poor substitute. I wanted to ask Amanda for advice, but I didn't know what our relationship was anymore, and I didn't want to risk upsetting Zoey further. As ridiculous as that was. I rubbed my chin with my hand and was dismayed to find I had missed a spot. I scratched irritably at the scruffy stubble and wondered if that was why Zoey hadn't taken me back.

* * *

I sat at the table closest to the door at Brad's, sipping on cranberry juice. I didn't feel like drinking. I stirred the drink with a straw and watched the ice cubes circle the perimeter of the glass. The bar was practically empty, it was only 10:00. No one really showed up until 12:00, 11:30 at the earliest. There was a lot more light now, so people could see their food. They would turn down the lights later so people couldn't see each other. I brushed my hair out of my eyes. I still hadn't cut it. I had been afraid Zoey wouldn't like me as much with shorter hair. I had bought a comb for the first time in my life. I rarely used it. I pulled at my NYU shirt, adjusting it. I could feel my armpits starting to sweat. It still hadn't rained, and the humidity was killing me. My umbrella stood propped against my chair. I touched it with my hand to make sure it was still there.

The door opened and I felt a cool breeze. Kevin walked in, Amanda trailing him. Kevin was wearing a white button-down with the sleeves rolled up, along with khaki pants and brown loafers. Amanda trailed him cautiously, wearing a sleeveless top with a flowery design and a short blue skirt. Her legs were tanned. I looked at my bare arms. They were a little tanned, but still very pale. I watched her as they sat down.

"Hello." I kept my voice neutral. Kevin looked at us nervously.

"You guys are cool, right?" He watched my face.

"Yeah," I said. Amanda relaxed.

"How's Zoey?" she looked at me sympathetically. Or maybe it was apologetically. I was finding it harder to read her these days.

"She's taking some time to figure out whether or not she trusts me." Kevin and Amanda couldn't hide their frowns. I knew how bad it sounded.

"Did you talk to her today?" Kevin, ever the pragmatist, wanted as much information as possible. I explained my visit to her apartment, emphasizing how apologetic I had been and how unreasonable her demands were. Kevin nodded at each of my points.

"I think you should wait, man. Give her space." He leaned back in his chair. He scanned the bar, eager to move on to more interesting activities. I agreed.

"You're both idiots." Amanda hadn't spoken at all while I talked. Now she leaned forward. I caught myself looking at the mole on her chest and consciously redirected my eyes to her face. "You love this woman, right?"

"Yes." I did love her, even if she was being unreasonable.

"And you want to be with her?"

"Of course."

"So why does it matter who's 'right' in this case?" She paused. I thought about it. "Oh, and by the way, she is absolutely correct. I would be furious if I caught my boyfriend hanging out with an ex without telling me first."

"But I would never cheat on her-"

"I get that." She cut me off. "You are an excellent boyfriend in many ways. But you're stubborn and can't empathize." I opened my mouth to protest.

"It's true man. You are stubborn, almost as bad as Brian was." Kevin chimed in.

"She's probably been cheated on before. A lot of girls have. That betrayal makes it hard to trust again."

"Her last boyfriend cheated on her a lot." I said this quietly. Amanda was hijacking what was supposed to be a man-to-man conversation about the mysteries of women. I sipped my cranberry juice.

"Exactly. And now you expect her not to react to you hanging out with me?" The question slapped me in the face. I shook my head. I started to get it, to realize how it looked. "Look, I'm not blaming you for us hanging out last night. I never should have agreed to be alone with you. I may still have some feelings for you, but that's my issue. You need to focus on making this right."

"I just want her to realize I would never cheat on her, and that she can't control me." I drummed my fingers on the table.

"She's not trying to control you, you moron." Amanda raised her voice. The black guys at the next table looked over. "If you care that much about winning this fight, you'll probably lose her. You won't ever remove that little nagging doubt in the back of her head. All you can do is not cheat on her, and treat her right."

"So what do I do now? Wait for her to think about it?" Kevin scratched his face and rested his head on his chin. He looked bored.

"No. The longer you let that fight sit, the more doubts she'll have. Her friends will tell her all men are scum, to forget about you. I know you made your dramatic speech and what-not, and Hollywood has taught you that that's all you can do. But it's not. Go talk to her. Don't confront her. Don't make some big romantic gesture. Explain to her that you realize why she's upset, and that you won't do anything like that again."

"Maybe you should talk to her, explain how we used to be friends-"

"You want her to think we talked about this? She already thinks we're too close. If you want to tell her that, fine. But don't make it sound like an excuse. Tell her unequivocally that you were wrong. And do it soon." Amanda leaned back. I nodded my head. It made sense.

"I'll do it." I started planning what I'd say and how I'd say it. Then I stopped. I needed to speak from the heart. Murph walked in and came over to our table. He said hello.

"Who wants to get drunk?" Kevin smiled. Amanda ran her hands through her hair.

"Me," she said. "I need to get laid." Kevin and Murph laughed. I looked at her. For the first time, I wondered about how she had dealt with breaking up with me, with Brian's death. He had been one of her best friends, I admitted to myself. He had been one of all of our best friends. I looked at Kevin and Murph, who had walked off to buy a pitcher. They had been there for me, even when I hadn't been there for them. I realized how insensitive I'd been. I started to say something, then stopped. The time for that had come and gone. I resolved to be a better friend. Murph came back with the pitcher.

"What's that you're drinking, Zach?" He nodded at my cranberry juice. I winced, knowing what was coming.

"Cranberry juice."

"What're you on your fucking period? Have a beer." I laughed. He handed me a cup. I didn't need to drink to drown out my feelings or ignore them, but I could drink to enjoy the company of a few close friends.

"You better get laid," I said to Amanda. "I don't want to end up walking home with you." She laughed.

"I think I'll be fine." She waved to two tourists that were standing at the bar. They looked European. I could tell from the tight shirts and wispy facial hair. They smiled at Amanda and began talking animatedly amongst themselves.

I had a few beers and took off early after buying a pitcher for our table. I had fun. Amanda left with one of the Europeans, and Kevin and Murph were talking to two very attractive black girls when I left. I wouldn't be missed. I thought of Zoey. I knew that we would get through this rough patch, that in a week everything would be fine. I just wanted that week to have passed, for everything to be right again. I fell asleep that night thinking of all the things I wanted to do with her.

Chapter 12

I strolled casually through the glass double doors and nodded to the security guard. He lifted his cap off his head and ran a wrinkled hand through his thick black hair. A phone rang. He picked up a black headset and began speaking in Spanish. I couldn't understand a word.

The walls of the lobby were a deep brown. I stepped onto an intricate rug, it reminded me of the rugs my mother used to have at our house when I was a kid. She had always yelled at my father and me for getting them dirty.

"They're on the floor. We're supposed to step on them," he'd say. She'd give him a look and he'd go quiet. He never spoke much.

I went over to the guard. I told him the name of Zoey's company, and asked what floor they were on. He told me without consulting a book or the monitor in front of him. He went back to talking in Spanish to whoever was on the other end of the line. He had a thick bushy mustache that moved up and down while he talked. I licked my lips, lamenting my inability to grow a mustache of any substance. Whenever I went a few days without shaving my upper lip, I looked like a pedophile.

I waited for the elevator. There was a large mirror in between the two shafts. I examined myself. I checked my armpits for sweat stains. I was relieved to find I had none. I was wearing a purple golf shirt that didn't stain easily. I pulled up my jeans as the bell rang to indicate that the elevator had come. I let the three women in suits, talking animatedly, pass in front of me out of the elevator, then stepped on. The doors closed, and I was alone in the silver metallic chamber. I pressed the six button, and it glowed orange. I waited patiently, watching the numbers on the display above the buttons count up as we rose. I jumped and my feet landed quicker than they should have. I'd been jumping on elevators since I was a little kid and I figured out that it changed how high you could jump. I used to do it no matter how many people were on the elevator, but now I only did it when I was alone. I figured that meant I was more mature, an adult now.

The doors opened on four. Two men got on. One was tall, the other short. The short one was much older. His curly gray hair bounced as he walked. The tall nervous one followed him, listening carefully to everything he said. I didn't understand a word of it. Quantum this and quantum that and quantum both. He might as well have been speaking Spanish to the guard downstairs.

We rose to six. The doors opened and the three of us got off. I hesitated. They turned left and walked quickly down the grey-carpeted floors and disappeared out of sight. I watched them. The walls were bare, and as white as could be. It felt like I was in a hospital. I looked for some sort of sign for which way to go. I didn't know her office number, or if she even had an office. I went left.

I heard people talking. I turned left at the end of the hallway. There was a conference room with the door slightly ajar. Zoey's voice carried out into the hallway. I peeked inside. She wore a black and white top and a knee-length black skirt. Her legs were perched on black open-toed heels. She was standing in front of a white board, arguing something with an older man with a beer belly and a large mole under his right nostril. She gestured impatiently at something on the board, and he made a Settle Down gesture with his hands.

"If we accept this as true-"

"But I don't believe that it is true-"

"But all the evidence-"

"Is inconclusive." Zoey stopped arguing. He was clearly her boss, or superior to her in some regard. She closed her mouth and glanced towards the door. I shot back. She hadn't seen me. I backed up and rested my back against the wall opposite the door. A maintenance man passed by and looked at me. He nodded to me. I looked at his wizened old face and imagined him as a young man, chasing girls and dreaming of a job that he never got. I wondered if he was happy. I nodded back and he continued on with his day. He'd never remember my face, we'd never see each other again. We were just two of the seven billion people on earth all fighting for the same thing; happiness. I wondered if it was possible for everyone to be happy. It seemed to me, at least in that moment, that it wasn't. There needed to be somebody who was sad, I reasoned, so that the happy people could have something to compare themselves to and realize they were in a better situation.

Zoey came out about fifteen minutes later. She looked frazzled. Her eyebrows raised when she saw me.

"I can't do this now," she said and started walking quickly down the hallway away from the elevators. I walked after her, dodging all the people walking in the other direction. Zoey cut a path through them easily as she walked, it was as if people just got out of her way. When I tried to follow, the path was closed and I had to swerve around the identical men in their identical khakis, white button-downs, and red ties. They all looked busy and were walking as fast as possible without running.

"There's nothing to do." She shushed me. We passed a water cooler. There was no one standing around it. Zoey grabbed a cup and filled it almost without breaking stride. "I'm not here to make a scene." She turned and looked at me. I had caught up to her and we walked side by side.

"Then why are you here, Zach?"

"I'm here to say I was wrong, and you were right." Zoey stopped. She smiled.

"More."

"I shouldn't have been hanging out with Amanda. Especially without you knowing. I see why you reacted the way I did and I'm sorry I didn't understand before." She kept walking.

"Turn here." She walked into a door with a stick figure wearing a dress on it. I barely noticed.

"I want us to get through this. I want you to trust me. I made a mistake, and I'm asking you to forgive me. Why are we in the bathroom?" I noticed the white tiled floors and the distinct lack of urinals.

A pair of sinks and mirrors showed her step closer to me. She passed from one mirror into the next. Mirror Zoey planted a kiss on Mirror Zach's lips.

"Are we…" She nodded. I kissed her back. We went into a stall and I struggled with the lock.

A few sweaty minutes later, Zoey was pulling her heels back on.

"So are we good?" I asked, panting. She stood up and kissed me on the cheek, rising to her tippy-toes to do so.

"We're getting there."

"Let me take you to dinner tonight." My tone was uncommanding. She considered it.

"Fine. Where shall I meet you?" She opened the stall and we exited.

"No, let me *take* you to dinner tonight. I'll pick you up at 8:00." She looked at me, her eyes twinkled.

"Alright, then, mister boss-man. 8:00 it is." She poked her head out the door. She stepped out and motioned for me to follow.

"Weren't you afraid we'd be caught?" I asked as I stepped out. The walls of the hallway were even whiter than those of the bathroom.

"You obviously don't realize how few women work here." She reached over and buttoned the top button of my golf shirt. "Now, get the hell out of here before I lose my job." I laughed.

"Which way?" She pointed me back down the hallway.

"And I'm this way." She walked backwards away from me, smiling. "I'll see you at eight."

"It's a date." I couldn't stop smiling. I strutted down the hall. On the way out of the building I nodded confidently at the guard.

"You find what you were looking for?" he asked, barely looking at me.

"Yes, thank you for your help." I don't think he realized the scope of his question.

* * *

I made a reservation at the finest Italian restaurant I knew. I went to the barber and got a haircut. I busted out the one suit I owned. I wore a black button-down with white stripes and a silver tie. I spent twenty minutes getting dressed, and twenty more admiring myself in the mirror. I brushed my teeth, taking care not to get any paste on my suit. It was a black suit that I owned and wore to all occasions. The big three: weddings, job interviews, and funerals. I had been to one of them recently and hoped to attend one of the others 9 to 12 months from now. I put the little black box with the soft velvet exterior in my front left pocket. I gave Mirror Zach a pep talk. He looked good. I rubbed my head and looked at the tiny hairs on my hand. I moved the ring to the front right pocket to see how it felt there.

I leaned over the sink and rubbed my head furiously with both hands. Tiny flecks of black appeared in the bone-white sink. I washed my hands, with my sleeves unbuttoned and rolled up. My jacket hung on the notch in the door normally reserved for my towel. My yellow towel lay on top of the toilet. I took the ring out. I practiced opening the case, revealing the diamond ring beneath. I practiced kneeling, not actually touching my knee to the ground to protect my black pants. I put the ring in the interior jacket pocket. I looked in the mirror again. I was twenty-five years old. I was ready to be a husband. Well, a fiancé at least. Nothing wrong with a long engagement.

I grabbed the jacket and slipped it on, looked in the mirror one more time, then went to grab my wallet, phone, and keys. I checked my phone. No new messages. My greatest fear was that Zoey would have to postpone, or cancel, and I'd have to go another day with the pit in my stomach. I had thirty minutes to kill before I had to go. I couldn't sit still. But I was no longer killing time until it was time to go kill time elsewhere. I was killing time to get to an important part of my life, and that was different. Better.

I sat on the couch. I patted my jacket to make sure the ring was there. I went into the kitchen. I moved the ring to my front left pocket, next to my keys. I tried it in the right pocket with my phone, that didn't feel right either. I settled on having it in my back left pocket, pressed tight against my upper thigh. I looked in the fridge. I wasn't hungry. I reached up to close the cupboard door, which had been left ajar. I felt the ring slide, I grabbed at my back pocket. That was out, I wasn't going to live with the constant fear of reaching into the pocket and not having a ring there.

I was sweating. That made me nervous I would look sweaty and gross, which made me sweat more. I dabbed at my forehead with a hand towel. I breathed deeply. I held the ring in my left hand and considered hiding it behind my back for the entirety of the meal. I texted Zoey. *Btw, make sure to dress nice.* A few minutes later, my leg buzzed. *When do I ever not?* I read the text from my possibly future fiancé and laughed. It wasn't really funny.

I bounced from one foot to the other. I went into the bathroom. I still looked fine. I shadow boxed my reflection, still clutching the ring in my left fist. I considered carrying it in my mouth like a squirrel carrying nuts. I decided against it. I checked the time, still ten minutes before I had to go. I left anyways, figuring I could just walk slowly.

I walked past Mrs. Johnson and her cat. I crept past, terrified of showing up at Zoey's apartment with orange hair all over my suit. We exchanged pleasantries. I considered how far I had come since my last wedding proposal. I hoped that this one would end better. I knew it would. It was a Monday night, after all, not a Wednesday. I had learned.

I put the ring in my left front pocket. I kept my left hand clutched around it as I walked. I noted again to myself how filthy Manhattan was. I wished I had a plastic bubble to prevent my suit from having even the faintest mark of dirt or hair or anything when Zoey saw me. I walked quickly, then reminded myself to walk slowly. A fellow suit wearer bumped past me. He glared at me. I stared at his receding hair-line and slight pot belly and imagined myself like that in fifteen years, with a few kids and Zoey. The thought didn't scare me. I whistled as I walked. Here comes the bride. I told myself to be less of a cliché. I didn't know how.

I rapped my knuckles on Zoey's door. She opened it immediately. I widened my eyes and snapped my head back, exaggerating my surprise at her quickness in answering the door. She widened her eyes and snapped her head back, exaggerating her surprise at my outfit.

"Wow." she smiled at me. She was wearing a dazzling silver gown, with four-inch black heels and a gold necklace. "Did I dress nicely enough?" She spun around in a circle. It was the last outfit she'd ever put on as a single woman. I hoped. I thought about which one of us would die first.

"Wow," I said. I stepped inside and kissed her.

"May I ask the occasion?" She went and got her purse.

"It's not every day you take the most beautiful woman in all the five boroughs to dinner." I grinned. She laughed at me.

"You are such a loser." She walked past me out the door. I followed like a puppy follows his new owner.

"What does that make you?" I shot back as we waited for the elevator.

"A generous citizen." I laughed. She shot me a look. Her green eyes flitted over to mine, then back. She was happy. I made her happy. "Nice haircut."

Chapter 13

"That really was an excellent meal, but I'm not sure why you brought me to such an expensive place," she said after the tall, dark, and handsome waiter had taken our plates away. "I hope all this isn't to make up for what happened."

I looked at her. She was intently focused on me. "It's not." I wiped my mouth with my napkin. I felt the ring with my left hand.

"Okay…" She trailed off, waiting for an explanation.

"My mother isn't right about a lot of things." I opened and closed the box with my thumb in the hidden recesses of my cheap suit. "But, uh, she was right about you." Zoey smiled and opened her mouth to respond. "I'm not finished. Please, I'm, well, I'm trying to say something to you. Just wait." She nodded.

"A few months ago, I hated the world. I drank and smoked and partied to avoid the fact that I was unhappy. Now, I, uh, well, I'm happier." I cursed myself in my head for stumbling over the words so much. "Not all of that is because of you, but you are a big part of it." Zoey seemed to understand what was about to happen. She put down her napkin on the table (the waiter was boxing up her leftovers for me to take home) and folded her hands.

"These past few days made me realize something: I… um, don't want to lose you. I can't stand the idea of it." TDH brought over the check. I thanked him. "I didn't want to believe that my mother would set me up with, well, the girl that…" I trailed off. Zoey put her folded hands over her mouth.

"Yes…" she said. She waited for me to get the words out.

"The girl that I would want to marry." She beamed from behind her hands. I got up and got down on one knee. The other people in the restaurant turned to watch. We had become a cliché, a good story they would tell to people who asked them how their dinners had been. I didn't care. I took out the little black box. Zoey stood up. I opened the ring.

"Zoey Mclemore," I paused. In that moment, I could see everything. The tiny wrinkles on her beautiful round face as she started to smile even wider, the tiny bob in her head as she started to answer the question before it could be asked. I saw behind her, saw through her. I saw the shy, doesn't-know-he's-handsome, young busboy precariously balancing several plates as he navigated through tables to deliver food to a few tables over from ours. I saw the elderly lady that was turning around, unaware she was about to knock the food from the poor kid's hands. I saw another waiter see the same thing I saw, and I saw the muscles in his leg twitch as he sped up to try and intercept the carnage. I saw TDH making his way over to our table, stepping on the red and gold carpet as he took the first of two steps up to our section of the restaurant. I saw his hand resting on the ornate wooden railing that helped patrons up the stairs and connected to a divider between our raised section of the restaurant and the rest of the building.

I saw the faces of all the other diners, as they watched the young couple that would remind them of what they had once had, or what they one day hoped to have. I saw the families with their kids, and I saw them looking on, their wide eyes and round cheeks displaying their innocence and inexperience. I saw the tiny speck of chicken parmesan that had found its way onto Zoey's gown. That slight imperfection that somehow amplified her beauty.

But more than that, I saw the future. Or a possible future. I saw the excited aftermath, the triumphant kiss that would lead, after months of planning, to another kiss. I saw the cheering of the other patrons that would morph into the cheering of our families and friends. I saw my mother, bragging for decades about setting me up with Zoey.

I saw our children, a little boy and a little girl. I saw them grow old before our eyes, as visitors remarked how much they had grown. I saw them go from children to thinking adults, saw them find others as we had found each other.

At the same time, I saw a darker possibility. Her answer was certain, but what would happen after was not. I saw us moving in together, I saw her displeasure at the state of the bathroom and me complaining about her hair being everywhere. I saw the resentment, the anger that would build. I saw her nagging me about cleaning up, and I saw myself nagging her about nagging me.

I saw us complaining to our friends, I saw my mother telling me she had never liked Zoey. I saw myself agreeing. I saw lawyers, and I saw tears. I saw an amicable separation, followed by years of writing checks to a woman I never saw. I saw that this was not the happy ending I had always wanted- I saw that this moment was a happy beginning, one that would take years of work and love and respect to nurture into a happy life, followed by the certainty of a sad ending. Because death is always the ending, not marriage, and death is always sad. I saw all this, and I considered. Is this what I wanted? I saw Zoey's smiling eyes and her gorgeous body, but more than that I saw the wonderful person that lay beneath. The kindness, the sense of humor, the understanding. I saw the mother of my future children, and I asked her,

"Will you marry me?"

About the Author

Ian Mark first dipped his toes into the writing waters as a high school senior when his essay equating college admissions with dating was published in Boston Globe Magazine. After a string of one-night standard applications he hooked up with NYU and spent the next 3 years immersed in Manhattan (and yes, sigh, occasionally Brooklyn) nightlife. He graduated Phi Beta Kappa and magna cum laude with a B.A in English and American Literature in 2015. Forgoing a lucrative career in… uh… Englishonomics maybe? Ian placed his degree somewhere he cannot remember and absconded to Pasadena, CA, where he hosts The Pasadonuts Improv Livestream every week and works as an actor in film and television. His writing has appeared in Hive Magazine, Outrageous Fortune, CelticsBlog, the Newton Tab, and Washington Square News.

He grew up in Newton, MA, where he perfected the art of faking illness to skip school and read novels all day. After reading a thousand or so he began imagining writing his own. After a hundred more he jumped in the deep end. This is his first novel. He has no children or pets. Follow him on Twitter @TheRealIanMark

www.ingramcontent.com/pod-product-compliance
Lightning Source LLC
Chambersburg PA
CBHW020520120726
47904CB00003B/905